THE PERFECT STORM

A MCLAUGHLIN SISTERS NOVEL (STRANDED IN
GETAWAY BAY ROMANCE, BOOK 1)

ELANA JOHNSON

AEJ
CREATIVE WORKS

ISBN-13: 978-1-63876-098-6

CHAPTER ONE

*E*den McLaughlin tucked her blonde hair behind her ear, the Hawaiian spring wind trying to whip it right off her head. Once she got around the corner up ahead, she'd get some relief.

If only she could get the same reprieve from her thoughts simply by rounding a corner. But no, they continued to go round and round even after she got away from the wind. Deciding to take a break, she found a level piece of ground on the trail she'd escaped to in the wilds of Hawaii—if such a thing could be found.

And it could. Getaway Bay was thriving and growing, but there were still plenty of off-the-beaten-path trails and hikes and opportunities on the island. Sure, she had to drive a little. Yes, hers was the only car in the parking lot—which was little more than a patch of dirt next to a non-marked trailhead.

But this kind of back-country exploring was what Eden thrived on. She sat down and pulled out the survival tool she'd jimmy-rigged to be everything she needed while hiking. Part knife, part can opener, part pair of scissors, it literally had everything—even a compartment for a solar blanket and a six-foot length of cord she could use for a dozen purposes.

And no one wanted it.

"Billionaires." She scoffed out the word as she pulled the portable stove from her pack. Another invention of hers, she could heat a single serving of whatever she wanted in something the size of a can of beans.

None of the billionaire investors that had flocked to Fisher DuPont's huge eyesore of a hotel on the beach wanted to give her any money to get her line of survival gear off the ground. Her latest meeting had been yesterday with a man named Darius Blood. Yes, Blood.

"More like blood*sucker*," Eden muttered as she got the container of chicken casserole from her pack and scooped it into the can. It had two bottoms, one of which was connected to the other with thin strips of metal, allowing her to stuff grass and small sticks into the gap between the two.

Using her multipurpose tool, which also held matches, she lit the debris and got the flame going. No need to just pack sandwiches anymore. The speeches she'd prepared for her products lingered in her mind, always just out of reach. Ready to be called upon, should she get asked a question in line at the grocery store or on an elevator.

After all, she understood the seven degrees of separation better than almost anyone, and it could be that the cashier could have a brother who knew someone, who knew who owned the biggest and most profitable survival company in Getaway Bay.

Explore Getaway Bay.

Eden had tried to find out who really owned the company. It seemed like every door that opened, five more closed—and she worked as a tour guide for the outdoor department of the company. And she still had no idea who really signed her checks.

Not that there were literally any checks to sign. Not in this digital age.

Sometimes Eden wanted to rewind time, go back to when she had to have cash to buy something, and everything passed from person to person. Now, people could buy whole islands with virtual money, and Eden didn't understand any of it. She loved the land, the island, the act of going outside and exploring.

And that was what she did, six days a week. Well, seven if her own exploration of Getaway Bay on her day off counted.

The ocean in front of her brought a small measure of comfort, and she watched the horizon, wondering how long it took for the water way out there to crash against the rocks on the cliffs below her.

Probably as long as it had taken Jeremy to know he

didn't want to see her again. She'd been on six first dates in the past couple of months, and she couldn't get a man to commit to a second.

Maybe she talked too much about her inventions. Maybe she didn't talk enough. She'd tried both and failed both times. She told herself it didn't matter, because between working in the shed in her backyard to make awesome outdoor products, her real day job, and all her investment meetings, she certainly didn't have time for a boyfriend.

She'd tried the app that had sent the island into a tailspin—Getaway Bay Singles—but she'd struck out there too.

Eden leaned her head back against the rocks, deciding this week just sucked and she needed to hang in there until next week.

Next week, she'd be on the submarine, her favorite tour, and that would make this week better. She had no more investment meetings, and she'd just take a break from the shed.

That all decided, she ate her chicken and rice, her mood lifted somewhat by the food and the plan to move forward. Still with her back against the cliff, she pulled out her phone and sent a group text to her sisters.

Maybe I don't understand men because I don't have any brothers.

The message went zipping through cyberspace, where it would land on her sister's phones. They'd send back condolences about Jeremy, who Eden had been very hopeful about. Then they'd throw in stories of their latest dating disasters, and Eden would offer to make dinner at her place that night.

She'd always felt a bit out of place among her sisters, but they were her best friends at the same time. She wasn't sure why her parents had gone for plant names for all of them, but she'd gotten Eden.

Orchid, Iris, Ivy—and Eden. It might have made sense if she was the baby of the family. Like the Garden of Eden. But nope. She was the second oldest, and the twins—Iris and Ivy—had just celebrated their thirtieth birthday.

The sky darkened, and Eden glanced up. Concern flowed through her, and she realized she'd been staring at her phone instead of paying attention to the weather. Things could shift suddenly out in the ocean, and she knew better than most. How many times had she said that to tourists coming through the office?

Thousands.

She hastily stood up and packed up her things, the first drops of rain already falling though the sun was still shining in parts of the sky. She'd climbed for a good hour before stopping, and it would be slick and hard to get down if the rain continued for very long.

Big, heavy drops kept pounding the ground around her, soaking her face and hair before she'd even shouldered her pack. What a perfect way to end this horrible week, and it felt like God and Mother Nature had combined forces against her.

She took a few steps to the corner and hesitated. Perhaps she should just stay here. One step into that wind, and she might blow away. Her calves burned from standing on the downward slope, but she couldn't see very far behind her to know if there was a cave or a small divot in the rocks where she could at least find some shelter from the storm.

Most storms like this raged for fifteen minutes or less, and if she could just wait it out, she'd have a much smoother hike back to her car.

Turning, she headed back the way she'd come, passing the flat spot where she'd eaten lunch. She kept one hand continually on the cliffs on her left, her situation growing more and more dire by the moment.

She finally stopped, unable to keep climbing due to the slope and the slippery mud the path had become. Feeling stupid—how lame would a headline look about one of Getaway Bay's top outdoor tour guides getting stuck in the wilderness?—she pulled out her phone and texted her sisters.

Stuck out a Bald Mountain Cliffs. If I don't call someone in an hour, send help.

Help? Orchid's text came right back, and Eden tried not to roll her eyes. Orchid never wore anything but heels, the thought of actually hiking a horrifying one.

Eden couldn't focus on the text string right now. She needed to get out of this rain. After zipping her phone back in her pants pocket, she turned back down the trail. Maybe she'd missed something, but it was pretty hard to tell.

In the end, she crouched down close to the face of the cliff and ducked her head as low as possible, covering it with her hands. The storm would just last a few more minutes. Microbursts. That's all Hawaii got, unless they'd already braced for a tropical storm or a hurricane. And there hadn't been anything on the weather report that morning.

She wasn't sure how long she crouched there, but it couldn't have been long—her knees didn't even hurt yet—before an awful, cracking, crashing, thundering sound filed the air. Filled her ears, her whole soul.

She gasped and lifted her head, trying to locate the source of the noise. But it echoed from everywhere, as if the sky itself had split open and the Earth would be ending in the next few seconds.

The warm rain pounded against her face, blinding her, and Eden ducked her head again, true fear flowing through her.

The ground beneath her began to shake, and she bolted to her feet.

"The mountain is coming down."

Sure enough, in that moment, Bald Mountain Cliffs started shedding off rocks like a snake does its skin. Eden had nowhere to go to escape—not this time.

She got swept away by the landslide as it rammed into her back, stealing her breath and shooting toward that corner she'd rounded. She knew the landslide wouldn't turn and follow the path, but go right off the side of the cliff.

And she was going with it.

She screamed as she fell, landing much sooner than she'd have thought. She rolled as more mud and rocks continued to rain down on her, pain flashing through her temples, her knees, her back, and her hands.

All at once, she found shelter from the rain and all the debris flowing over the path above. She drew in a shaky breath, the edges of her vision turning white.

"I'm going to pass out," she murmured, glad she'd texted her sisters.

"Hey," a man said, and Eden jerked toward the voice. Bad move. Her head swam, and she couldn't see very well at all.

She groaned and started to tip forward, the man catching her in his arms at the same time he said, "Eden?"

Eden looked up in the gorgeous, if not a little bloody, face of Holden Holstein. Ah, Holden. This was a nice dream. One where he held her in his arms, kissed her, shared his deepest sorrows with her.

"Are you with me?" he asked, and Eden's eyes snapped open again. "Don't pass out, Eden."

But she couldn't hold on. Of course Holden—the one and only man she'd ever loved—would have to be in this cave. Had to be a witness to her falling off a cliff and passing out.

"Holden," she murmured. She'd wanted to say so much to him before they'd broken up all those years ago. But she couldn't then, and her tongue was too thick and her brain too slow now.

So she settled into the warm darkness, the scent of Holden's skin and cologne lulling her right into unconsciousness, the way it had so often in the past.

CHAPTER TWO

*H*olden Holstein couldn't really hold Eden's weight, though she was a tall, lithe woman with hardly any body fat. But a rock had landed on his leg, and he was pretty sure it was fractured.

He laid Eden down as gently as he could, but he was pretty sure she groaned as he did. It was hard to tell above the pounding rain just a few feet away, and all that mud, foliage, and rock falling off the ledge up above.

He couldn't believe he'd picked today to come out here. It literally hadn't rained in Getaway Bay in a month, and he'd thought the wet season had ended. It was the middle of May, and the weather usually played nice by now.

Holden fell to the ground beside Eden, panting now that the adrenaline had worn off. Pain pulsed through his leg, and it would be a miracle if he got out of here alive. Of course, he would. If the hardships Holden had already endured in his life hadn't killed him, this landslide wouldn't.

At least he'd told Dean where he was going. Of course, his advisor at Explore Getaway Bay knew everything about Holden. Everyone thought Dean was the brains, brawn, and billions behind the survival company, outdoor tours from underwater to the top of the dormant volcano, and mega-online resource for wilderness survival.

Holden had brought his phone with him. At least Eden had a backpack on. He glanced at her, noticing that she was wearing an Explore GB T-shirt, and guilt spread through him like wildfire.

She worked for his company, and surely she could get them out of this mess. But he hated that he couldn't do it. Hated that he owned the company but couldn't tell Eden. Couldn't survive in the wilds of Hawaii by himself. Hated that he'd lost Eden years ago.

But his mother had been dying, and he hadn't been able to deal with the demands of a relationship too. Even though Eden hadn't been a demanding girlfriend, Holden simply hadn't been in a place where he could keep her.

So he'd cut her loose. He'd cut a lot of people and things loose during that difficult time of his life, and he'd been slowly putting pieces back together since then.

Privately. Behind closed doors.

His half-brother had taken over their father's cattle ranch and become a billionaire himself. Holden had been building his wealth through selling flashlights, emergency blankets, and rations to the hikers and outdoor enthusiasts that came to Getaway Bay to see some of the world's most amazing sights.

He worked closely with Dean Black, a childhood friend who'd stuck with Holden through all the ups and downs of his family life. When he tried to explain to people how he was younger than his half-brother, but that his dad was married to Lincoln's mother...it hurt his own head.

Shaking the thoughts from his head, he told himself to focus. He didn't need a family history lesson right now. He needed to stay awake so there wouldn't be two unconscious bodies under this ledge.

He reached over and covered Eden's hand with his. She wasn't cold, which was a good sign, but she didn't move either. Bad sign.

"Mom, what do I do here?" When he got really stressed, talking to his mother was the best thing to do. After his dad had gone back to his previous wife, leaving Holden and his mother, they'd relied on each other for so much.

"I just wanted an afternoon away," he said. "Dean says there's this new app service, and our company needs it. People can schedule their tours right from their phones. See availability. All of that. He says I should negotiate with Theo, because I already work there, and he thinks I could code the app myself. Get a deal on the design."

Holden stopped talking, because it was way past time for Explore Getaway Bay to have an app, and he knew it. His mother couldn't really help him with this.

No, what he wanted help with was Eden.

It had been five years since they'd been a couple. Five years since his mother's illness. Five years since the funeral.

He'd thought of her every day since then, and while he'd blocked some memories from that time of his life and he knew he'd acted badly, he couldn't help hoping she'd come back to him.

Walk into his office one day and ask him to lunch.

Of course, she wouldn't do that. Couldn't even do that. Theo's offices were in a luxury condo building that required a code to get in. He'd known Eden was on his payroll, but he didn't really know the day-to-day details of her job. He didn't have to know. He owned Explore Getaway Bay on paper only, consulting with Dean every Monday and working at The Web Developer the rest of the week.

The rain beyond the ledge eased up, and Holden rolled toward the opening to see the water was definitely slowing down. A few feet of debris had piled up outside the ledge he'd found only a minute into the downpour. If he had anything besides his two hands, he could probably dig them out, even with the damaged condition of his leg.

As it was, he couldn't get himself to move. So he cupped his hand around Eden's again, closed his eyes, and evened out his breathing. If there was anything he'd learned growing up on the cattle ranch for a few years, it was to breathe through the pain.

His phone beeped, but it wasn't the notification for a text or a missed phone call. It was his battery notification telling him his phone was almost dead. He didn't even open his eyes. When he didn't respond to Dean's texts and calls, his best friend would call the cops.

And Eden had a whole slew of people who cared about her. They wouldn't be stuck up here forever.

She groaned, and Holden's eyes flew open. "Eden," he said, and her hand shifted away from his. "Wake up." He wasn't sure if he was telling himself or her. Using his hands, he pushed himself up and looked down at Eden.

She had beautiful blonde hair—at least when it was washed and curled. Even if she had it in its customary ponytail, he liked it. Right now, it was filled with mud, and Holden reached down and plucked a small stick out of it.

Her freckles stood out on her pale face, and Holden traced his fingertips along her chin. Her eyes fluttered open, and he knew if she did that, he'd be looking into the blue-green depths of the ocean.

"Eden, honey," he said. "Can you wake up?" I need your help. Please don't make me carry you out of here on a broken leg.

She groaned again, and he kept talking. "Eden, you need to wake up. We're stuck up on the cliffs, and I'm pretty sure if you don't get us out of here, they're going to have to call in rescue workers."

He almost smiled, but he absolutely could not allow that to happen. He didn't need his face splashed all over the newspapers, and people asking questions, and everyone assuming that computer nerds couldn't take care of themselves in the wilderness.

"Holden?" Eden's voice sounded like she'd gargled with rocks, but her eyes opened, and she focused on him.

"Hey." Maybe he said it a little too softly. Or maybe his leg hurt a lot, and he wasn't thinking clearly. "You fell off a ledge."

She tried to sit up, but pain flashed across her face, and she laid back down.

"Yeah, don't move," he said. "You literally fell off a ledge. I'm not sure how far up it was, but you passed out pretty dang quick, so I'm guessing you hit your head pretty hard."

She shifted, her eyebrows crinkling together. "Can you move my backpack? It's killing me."

"Sure, yeah." Holden quickly pushed the straps off her shoulders and pulled it out from under her. "What do you have in here? Anything good?" The darkness beyond the ledge didn't settle him, and he wondered if they'd get off the mountain before dark. At this rate, he didn't think so.

Eden grabbed it away from him with surprising strength and speed. "I—nothing." Their eyes met, and Holden felt the same attraction to her that had always existed between them. He thought about the first time they'd met, while she was a waitress at a place where everyone wears roller skates. She'd only been there for six months, just to pay off the last of one of her sister's funeral bills from the death of her husband.

She'd done it anonymously, and he wasn't sure if she'd ever told Orchid what she'd done.

He'd known her in high school, but she was a couple of years behind him, and he'd been quiet and kept to himself then too.

"I'm sorry," he said, a spasm of pain making his hands shake. He wiped his face, the spot of blood from the cut on his forehead dry now. It stung, but nothing hurt as much as his leg. "Got any painkiller in that pack?"

"Yes," Eden said in a hoity toity voice. "Of course."

"You should take some."

"Don't tell me what to do, Holden," she said, throwing him a nasty glare. So she wasn't going to play nice, even in this precarious situation. Holden hadn't realized how much he'd hurt her until that very moment.

"I won't," he said.

She shook the bottle of pills into her hand, the rattling noise making Holden's nerves scream at him. She took out a bottle of water—Holden didn't even have that—and swallowed them before looking at him again.

Her eyes went to his forehead, and he watched the concern march across her face. "Here." She handed him the bottle, and he shook four pills into his hand and swallowed them dry.

"Thanks," he said. "What else hurts? Anything broken?"

She started to move her limbs, and they all seemed to work, though she did flinch in pain the tiniest bit. "I don't think anything's too bad. My right ankle hurts a lot."

"You probably landed on it when you came shooting over the ledge with the landslide."

"Is that what happened?"

"Yeah." Holden looked at her. "I'd ducked under here, but I thought I heard someone screaming, so I was stumbling out, and that's when you appeared." Like an angel, out of the storm and the mud.

"Thank you for catching me before I fell," she said softly.

"Yeah, sure," he said again. He wondered how many more times he'd say it, and he told himself not to utter it again.

She shifted on the hard rock as the rain started to fall again, and Holden couldn't help his sigh. He tried to move, but a white hot flash of pain sliced through him, and he sucked in a breath and said, "Oh."

He hoped he could just play it off on the rain, but Eden was smarter than that. She always had been. She had a real mind, one she used and one he admired.

"What's wrong?" she asked.

"Nothing," he said, but he didn't even believe himself.

"Holden."

He'd always loved it when she said his name, but not this time. Not when it was laced with danger and warning.

"My leg is jacked up," he said. "What about you?"

"We already talked about me," she said, her eyes sliding down to his legs. "Which one?"

"Right."

She moved, and he drew in his breath through his teeth, making a hissing noise.

"I don't want you to touch it," he said.

"I have to touch it."

"It's broken," he said. "No one needs to touch it to know that." Every muscle in his body screamed at him to make sure she didn't touch his leg. But she kept inching that way, and Holden felt like he always did when he was with Eden—like he was trying to hold back the tide. And he hadn't been able to hold on last time.

He didn't think he ever would.

"Eden," he said, but he clearly didn't have the

warning voice down the way she did, because she just looked at him with those teal eyes and focused back on his leg.

"I'm going to move your pantleg," she said.

He tried to grip the rocks behind him, but they were slippery and smooth, and he still ground his teeth together as she pushed the fabric up to look at his leg. His skin was dirty, and a flash of embarrassment squirreled through him.

She paused and rummaged through her backpack, pulling out a package of wet wipes. "I'll be gentle, but I can't tell if the skin is broken."

"My bone isn't poking out," he said, almost rolling his eyes. Eden was always so careful, and this examination could take an hour.

So what? he asked himself. He had nowhere to go, as the rain continued to fall beyond the ledge. At least no more of the mountain was coming down.

The pressure on his leg made him yell out, and she immediately pulled back. "Sorry."

"I really don't think this is necessary," he growled.

"We could be up here for a while," she said. "Especially if you can't walk."

"I can walk," he said, not really knowing if that were true.

"Holden."

"Eden," he said in the same reprimanding tone.

She sighed like he was being difficult on purpose. "Just lay back."

"Fine, but can you hurry?"

"I'll try." She wasn't a great liar, and she didn't hurry. She cleaned his leg despite all his hissing, and she probed around with a couple of chilly fingers, finally saying, "I don't think it's broken. I think it's really badly bruised."

"You think so?"

"Got hit by a rock, right?"

"How did you know?"

"You have a massive lump on your leg, and it's really red." She pulled his pantleg back down and leaned over him. "Are you—?"

Holden looked up at her, wishing they were lying on the beach, the sun shining gloriously overhead, and she was about to kiss him.

"Am I what?" he asked, but she still didn't answer.

CHAPTER THREE

*E*den's mind had blanked when she'd looked into Holden's dark eyes. He wasn't glaring, so they weren't black, and he wasn't about to kiss her, so they weren't the storm cloud gray she enjoyed so much.

It was entirely unfair that he could be so handsome while covered in dirt and mud and blood. She cleared her throat and took out another wet wipe to clean up his forehead. As she did, the wound started to bleed a little bit. "This is going to need stitches," she said, bottling up her emotions.

This was Holden Holstein. She knew exactly who he was, and what kind of power he held over her heart. He had the ability to shatter it into a thousand pieces, and she was still trying to find all of the shards from last time, thank you very much.

"Do you have any supplies?" she asked, peering at him.

"No," he admitted. "I was just coming for a couple of hours."

"That's what everyone says," she said, wishing she'd packed more food. But she was just coming for the afternoon too. She'd happened to pack lunch, and her backpack always had high-protein and calorie dense snacks in it.

"How long do you think we'll be out here?" he asked.

"I thought it would just rain for a few minutes," she said.

"It did," he said. "It quit for a while, and then started up again."

"It wasn't supposed to rain today," she said. "I checked the weather." She waited for him to make some crack about how of course she had. But he didn't. She realized that he only did that when they were together, when he was teasing her, when he could kiss her afterward.

Her face grew hot, and she didn't dare look at him. He'd always had a way of being able to see what she was thinking, and he'd told her she wore everything on her face. She'd tried to hide things the way he did, but she simply didn't know how.

The rain tapered off and stopped again, and Eden started to stand. Her back cried at her to *go slower!* She did, and she managed to stand all the way up and stretch the aches and pains from her legs and back and neck. "I'm going to go see what we're dealing with."

"Be careful," he said, an urgency in his voice and on his face. So maybe he wasn't as great at hiding things as he used to be. Or maybe he didn't want to be all alone with no supplies. No matter what, Eden took precious seconds to put her backpack on so if she fell again, she'd at least have her phone, her snacks, and all the other stuff she'd brought with her.

She felt bad for Holden, but there was no way he was walking out of here. She'd either shoulder most of his weight down, or rescue hikers would be coming in to get him. That much was clear.

No, his leg wasn't broken, but he was in a great deal of pain and couldn't put any weight on his leg.

Outside of the ledge, the air held so much water it almost choked her when she breathed. It wasn't raining, but the humidity was off the charts. The small space outside the half-cave was full of debris, and she couldn't go more than a step or two without meeting mud.

She didn't want that on her shoes or back in the cave, so she stalled. To her left was open air, something dripping from the path above—where she'd come from. She looked up and judged the distance to be maybe fifteen feet or so.

Shivers racked her body, and she looked away. Her situation could be so much worse, and she was glad she couldn't look over the edge to see how much further she could've fallen. And what were the chances of finding another person and a cave in the span of ten seconds?

And not just any person.

"Holden Holstein," she whispered. The very man who'd plagued her for years. She sighed, half-relieved she wasn't stuck out here alone and half-annoyed she'd have to share her supplies with him.

To her right, another ten feet of ledge remained, and she carefully stepped that way, testing each section of rock to make sure it would hold her weight before committing to it. "The path is gone." Even through the dim light, she could see the path Holden had come up, on the other side of a twenty-foot gap.

Even with two good legs, neither of them could make that jump. She didn't have the right equipment to rock climb, though she was experienced in it. Holden had been too, at some point. After his mother's death, he'd finished his computer science degree and gotten a job with The Web Developer, one of Theodore Fleming's tech companies that had come to the island a few years ago.

It was Theo's dating app that Eden had tried and failed with. As far as she knew, Holden didn't use the app, but she couldn't know for sure. Anyone could choose any screenname, and she could've communicated with him in the brief time she'd used the app.

But somehow, she didn't think so. Holden was a

man of few words, and he didn't seem like the type to chat through an app with strangers.

Eden wished she didn't taste bitterness on the back of her tongue when she thought about Theo. Yes, she knew him. She'd pitched him her line of survival gear a few months ago, and he'd started shaking his head before she'd even finished the first sentence.

"I'm in technology," he'd said. "This is physical products."

"Maybe I could start selling with an app," she said.

He'd smiled and said, "Our apps are very expensive."

And that had been that. Eden had left his office feeling like a fool, and she'd vowed never to approach another billionaire looking for money. Then she'd gone and done it again.

Well, she'd learned some lessons, hadn't she?

Don't repeat the same mistakes.

She turned back to the cave, where Holden waited for a report on their situation. He was definitely a mistake she was not going to make again.

But she didn't want him to die in that cave, either. She moved back inside, glad that the interior of the cave felt so much more secure than the ground outside. "We're not getting out of here without help," she said. "There's nothing to the left—the landslide wiped everything out in that direction. And there's a huge gap in the path going back down. There's this, oh, I don't know."

She blew her breath out, trying to make mental calculations. "We've got about twenty feet across, and eight outside of the cave, most of it covered with mud and shrubs and rocks. We might be able to clear it, but I don't know why we would."

Depression lanced through her, but she might as well finish. "And this cave, which is what? Fifteen feet back? So twenty feet by twenty feet." Four hundred square feet. Her bedroom was bigger, and she didn't have to share it with her ex-boyfriend.

"Not only that," she continued when Holden said nothing. "But we have half a bottle of water between us, and…." She yanked open the zipper on her backpack and pulled out the plastic zipper bag where she kept the snacks. "And maybe one meal each."

She met his eyes, but it was too hard to look at him for long. Too many memories. Too many things left unsaid.

Glancing away, she stuffed the protein bars and single-serving bags of nuts back in her pack. "If it rains again, I'll set the bottle out to collect the water. I have a can as well. We can survive for several days without food, but not without water."

"Several days?" Holden asked, the first words he'd spoken since she'd returned.

"Holden, there is no direct path to where we are. We're on the side of a cliff, and no one knows where we are."

"I'll call Dean."

"I already texted my sisters," she said. "Let me call them and see if they can get someone to come help right away."

Holden put his phone to his ear too, but Eden wasn't going to let him be the only one to call. She'd told her sisters if she didn't call within the hour to send help, and they needed more information.

"My phone's dead anyway," he said. "Maybe I can use yours after you call Iris."

"How did you know I was going to call Iris?" She paused in her tapping, now wanting to call Orchid instead. But Orchid was probably already crying, and Eden didn't want to deal with that right now.

She saw she had twenty-seven new texts, but she ignored them and tapped Iris's number while Holden said, "You always call Iris," in a voice barely loud enough to hear.

"Eden," Iris said, heavy relief in her voice. "Ivy, it's Eden. Where are you? Do you need help?"

"Yes," Eden said. "We need help."

"We?" Iris said—another reason Eden called her. She picked up on little details.

"Yes," Eden said, working very hard not to clear her voice. "I'm here with Holden Holstein, and he can't walk."

"I can walk," Holden said at the same time Iris squealed and said, "Holden Holstein?" in the loudest voice possible. Leave it to her flirty little sister to focus on who Eden was stranded with instead of the fact that she was *stranded on a mountain* with the man who'd broken her heart.

"We have very little food and water," Eden said. "I brought several of my inventions, but they won't make food out of mud and rock."

"Where are you?" Iris asked.

"I parked just past mile marker forty-six," she said. "There's a path across the highway that leads up to the Bald Mountain Cliffs. I went up about an hour or so. We're in a little cave just below that path." She twisted toward Holden. "I'm not sure how Holden got here."

"I parked at the entrance to Cowboy's Beach," he said.

Eden knew the place. "His truck—" She looked at him, and he nodded. "Is at Cowboy Beach. He must've taken the trail that goes north from there. It comes up this way. But Iris, it's out. There's a huge gap in the path near where we are. I've got flags in my backpack, and I'll set them out in the morning."

"The morning? You're going to stay there overnight?"

As much as Eden didn't want to, she knew there was no way they were getting down tonight. "Yes," she said, meeting Holden's eye and holding it this time. "We'll have to stay here overnight."

CHAPTER FOUR

*H*olden's mood worsened with every passing hour. When Eden offered him a protein bar for the fifth time, he declined it—for the fifth time.

Eden leaned into his personal space, her eyes sparking in the darkness. Semi-darkness, as she had a flashlight in her pack. And an emergency blanket. Though the rain had cleared, Holden still felt a chill running through his bones.

Eden said it was shock. Eden said he had to drink something. Eden glared at him and growled, "You're eating this if I have to stuff it in your mouth and move your jaw for you."

Holden glared right back. "I'm fine."

She looked like she'd do exactly what she'd threatened to do, those eyes blazing at him like blue fire. Finally, she just fell back against the rocks where they'd moved once she'd declared they'd have to stay the night.

At least.

He hadn't missed those words.

He had a shareholder meeting in the morning that Dean had told him over and over about. Holden couldn't miss it—and yet, he was going to miss it.

A few hours had passed, and he and Eden hadn't spoken much. The drugs were starting to wear off, and his leg throbbed again, but he said nothing. He wasn't going to take all of Eden's medication, her food, and her water.

It had rained again, and she'd filled her bottle, her can, and a plastic container she claimed she'd brought food in. So they'd live. Holden may not know all the ins and outs of survival, but he knew enough. They had shelter and water, with a little bit of food.

"I'm sorry I didn't come to your mother's funeral," she said, breaking the silence between them. And wow, she shattered it.

Holden turned toward him, true surprise tugging against his heart. "It's okay."

"No," she said, almost before he finished speaking. "It's not okay. I should've been there. I know it was a hard time for you, and you needed a friend." She looked at him. "I—I just couldn't."

He reached over and slipped his hand into hers. "I didn't even want to be there, so I get it." He moved his hand back to his own leg. "Maybe we should turn out the light. Save it if we need it."

"Good idea." She leaned forward and clicked off the flashlight before stowing it in her pack.

True darkness enveloped them, and Holden stayed sitting up against the hard rocks. Eden adjusted her backpack right next to him and laid down beside him, the silver emergency blanket crinkling in the blackness.

"Pull it over you," she said.

"It's not that cold."

"I'm cold," she said. "Is this okay?" She snuggled right into his side, her head near his thigh.

"Fine," he said, pulling the emergency blanket over his legs. He wasn't cold, and with her beside him, he was sure he'd be plenty warm. Just the thought of her so close made his blood run hotter.

It was so much easier to talk to her in the dark, and he distracted himself from his growling stomach by saying, "Tell me about that can cooker."

One of the best things about Eden was her ability to talk. She told him about the cooker, as well as several other inventions she'd created in the shed in the corner of her backyard. She'd always been inventive, a thinker, and he enjoyed the gentle cadence of her voice.

"What about you?" she asked. "You're working for The Web Developer now, right?"

"Yeah," he said.

"You've always loved computers."

"I have," he said. "It's a good job. Keeps me away from the ranch."

"Still no solution for that?" Eden shifted, her hand landing on his knee. Holden liked it there, where it made his leg tingle in a good way.

"Lincoln is...Lincoln," he said. "And my father is my father. Without my mom, it's just me. Well, I have friends."

"Mm," Eden said, and Holden had heard that noise before. Many moons ago, sure. But he'd heard it. She was nearly asleep.

"So I build custom websites now," he said. "I like it, and it keeps me busy." The pay was good, and Theo allowed him the flexibility he needed to run Explore Getaway Bay too. Of course, Theo didn't know that was what Holden was doing. No one did, and he found himself wanting to share the secret with Eden.

He didn't, and the silence between them was comfortable. "You're still doing the tours?" he asked.

"Yeah," she said sleepily. "I work for Explore Getaway Bay. I rotate all over the island."

He suddenly wished he'd been more hands-on with the outdoor tour aspect of his own company. "Which one is your favorite?"

"The underwater submarine," she said.

"Why?"

"There's a lot of families and kids that do it. They aren't loud and obnoxious, like some of the whale watching expeditions. Even the hikes to the falls can have rowdy guys sometimes."

Holden nodded, though there was no way for her to see him. "Hmm," he added.

Several minutes passed, and he was sure she was asleep. He let his hand drift over her hair, but it was caked with mud and not exactly the romantic gesture he'd been hoping for.

Hoping for.

Don't be a fool, he told himself. Just because Eden was talking to him and being nice didn't mean she was willing to forgive him. She wouldn't take him back. He knew her, and she felt things deeply. Loved deep.

Hurt deep.

He did too, which was why they'd gotten along so well in the beginning. It was also the reason he'd distanced himself from her as he went through his mother's health decline and subsequent death. He didn't need to hurt Eden too, and he didn't even know how to deal with his own grief.

"I got help," he whispered to the darkness, to the wilds of Hawaii. She'd left her bottle and can and container out on the ledge, just in case it rained in the night, and he wished he had a drink. But he didn't dare move.

"I saw someone," he said. "A grief counselor. And I got better. I go back sometimes." He needed to go see Dr. Osthmus again. He could feel the darkness gathering way down deep in his soul, and if he rooted it out fast enough, it didn't take over his life.

"And I have friends. Dean Black. Remember him?" Of course Eden would remember Dean. They'd spent time together the last time Holden and Eden had dated.

He finally fell asleep too, something he'd thought impossible. He woke to the sound of dripping water, and he opened his eyes to try to locate the source of it. His throat hurt, and his back ached, and someone had positively stuffed a live coal in his leg.

The darkness felt like a living, breathing thing, and he couldn't even see his hand in front of his face. There was no pressure against his leg. No warmth. "Eden?" he whispered.

The dripping continued, and he realized it was rain. But the water was hitting something...unnatural. Through the sound of it, he heard a soft snore, and he knew Eden was still here.

More relief than he should've felt filled him, and he pushed away from the rocks with a groan. If it was raining, he could drink and set the bottle to refill. What he couldn't do was stumble out onto that ledge in the pitch blackness.

He'd turned off his phone when it was close to dying, but he powered it up now just to get a little light. Get the layout of where he was. See if Eden was still asleep on her pack. If not, he'd take her flashlight and get a drink.

His phone made a horrible chiming sound as it

turned on, the high-pitched dinging and singing filling the cave and echoing around for a long time. Still Eden didn't stir.

With the six percent of battery life he had left, he shone his screen around until it landed on Eden, several feet to his left. The pack was beside her head, and Holden strained to reach for it.

A couple of fumbled attempts later, he had the bag in his hands as he searched for the flashlight. His need to drink felt almost insatiable, and his tongue stuck to the roof of his mouth. With the light ready now, all he had to do was stand up and walk.

He'd told her countless times that he could walk. He would absolutely not allow himself to be carried down this mountain by her or anyone else.

He'd already been in the Getaway Bay gossip mill enough over the years.

He aimed the flashlight out into the darkness, easily finding the glinting plastic in the beam. The can sat next to it, but the container was nowhere to be found. A click later, and darkness enveloped him again. He put his left hand against the wall and pushed himself onto his knees.

His right leg cried out in pain, and he stilled, panting through the agony. It subsided slightly, and he bent his left leg and leaned against the wall, using it for security as he got to his feet.

Or rather, his foot.

Balancing all his weight on his left leg, his right

simply throbbed a warning at him. If he could lean into something, he could probably walk, but there was no wall leading out to the water.

"Come on," he told himself, thinking of those hot summer days when his dad would make him go out into the fields to move the pipes around. He'd worked through pain before. He could do it again.

Balancing a tiny bit of weight on his right toe, he managed to shuffle forward a few inches. He clicked on the flashlight and studied the ground to make sure he wasn't going to twist an ankle or shuffle into a rough part of the floor.

Foot by foot, minute by minute, he got closer to the water. He was walking, and he half-wished Eden were awake to see it.

A whistling sound alerted him to the fact that the wind had arrived, and he hesitated before taking another step. Probably two more, and he could crouch down and reach out and get the bottle.

It wobbled in the wind as he took another toe-step. Panicked that it would blow over and be lost forever, he stepped again quickly.

A cry tore through his throat as his leg buckled underneath him. He went down hard on his knees at the same time the bottle tipped. The same time the flashlight skittered out into the rain.

He reached for the bottle, desperate to be ninja-like in this moment. "Holden?" Eden asked from behind him, and everything happened so fast.

The bottle fell over, dumping it's contents on the already soaked rock. The flashlight went out. Behind him, the crackling, crinkling sound of the blanket meant Eden had gotten up.

"Holden," she said now, panic in her voice.

"I'm trying to get a drink," he said, his hand scrambling around where the bottle had been. He had to get it. They'd already lost one container. "The plastic container was gone. I was just so thirsty, and now the bottle's tipped."

A glow filled the cave, and Eden used her cell phone to approach him. "Why didn't you wake me up?" She switched on her phone flashlight and swept the ledge.

The bottle was gone.

Holden groaned as she reached out and collected the can. "Here, drink." She stepped back into the rain and collected the flashlight while Holden did as she said.

"I'm sorry," he said. "The wind blew it away."

"Whatever, Holden," she said as if she didn't believe him. "It doesn't matter now."

CHAPTER FIVE

*E*den watched Holden gulp the rainwater, and she probably should've stopped him. She was thirsty too. But she didn't. When he finished, he stuck his hand out in the rain and set the can back out to collect more. The steady sound of water hitting metal was loud enough to hear out here, and Eden really hated that.

"I've learned everything I could my whole life to survive in the wilderness," she said. "But in my head, I always had more supplies."

Holden gave a dark chuckle. "At least you have supplies at all."

"You need to eat."

"I'll eat when we get back."

"I have six packages of nuts. You can have one. Or two. It'll be fine." She couldn't know that, but she knew what Holden was like when he got hungry. He did stupid things, like try to walk to get a drink when he should've just woken her. She'd take an empty belly over a hangry Holden Holstein.

He lay on the rocks, his chest heaving and his eyes closed. Eden shone the flashlight, which flickered in an unsettling way, into the backpack and pulled out the bottle of pills.

"Holden," she said, trying to soften her voice. Orchid had mentioned that maybe the reason Eden couldn't get a second date was because she came on too strong. She was too loud. Laughed too much. Knew everyone on the island—sometimes even tourists.

She crouched next to him and held out four pills. "I need you to take these."

"I'm okay," he said.

He really was the stubbornest man on the planet. "Holden," she said again, getting even closer to his face. He smelled like earth and rain, with a hint of that musky cologne somewhere in his skin.

"Sweetheart," she said, and his eyes flew open and locked onto hers. "I'm really worried about you. Please take these pills." She inched her hand closer to him, hoping she could hold his gaze for as long as it took.

She *was* worried about him. Maybe she shouldn't have called him sweetheart, but it had gotten his attention.

"And your stomach will hurt if you don't eat just a little something with the meds. Please." Apparently, she wasn't above begging. She couldn't live with his pain—or his death—on her conscience.

"Okay," he said, groaning as he moved into a sitting position, both legs out in front of him.

"And I want to look at the leg again."

"There's nothing you can do," he said.

"If it's infected, I can drain it," she said.

"You will do no such thing."

"I have a knife," she said, slipping her hand into her pocket to pull her tool out. She reached for the can, which had begun filling with rainwater, and handed it to him. "Take the pills, please."

He did, and Eden counted it as a major win. She got out a bag of nuts and handed them to him. "Eat as many as you can stomach. You're probably dehydrated, and you might be sick with how much you just drank."

Holden's eyes shone like liquid ink, black and deep and mysterious. She'd seen those eyes when they were half-closed, filled with desire, about to kiss her. She'd seen them when they held nothing but anguish. Heartache. Loss.

She'd seen them crinkle when he laughed, and as she edged toward his leg, she wanted to see the range of his emotions in those gorgeous eyes again.

Her heart skipped a beat, a clear warning to her that if she let Holden Holstein back into her life, she'd be asking for trouble.

She sliced a slit in his pantleg before he could

protest, and then she didn't have to move his leg to see it. "Okay," she said. "That wasn't so hard, was it?"

"Hmm," he said, but he was eating the nuts, and Eden prayed for a third miracle that night. No infection. Or if there was one, that she could drain it and make sure he didn't lose his leg on Bald Mountain Cliffs.

She shined the flashlight on his leg and sucked in a breath at the angry, red skin. "Holden," she said, her voice reverent and scared. She gently touched the bump, which was about the size of a dinner plate at this point.

His skin was on fire.

"This is definitely infected."

"Eden," he said, his leg twitching, and he probably didn't even know it. "There's nothing you can do. Help will be here in the morning. I'm fine."

He was not fine, and Eden pulled her backpack over to her and started rummaging around inside it. She had a little case full of items. Safety pins. Bandaids. Ointment. Flossers. Quarters, back when there were pay phones. Aspirin.

And she was sure she had some antibiotics. "I had these pills once," she muttered. "They were yellow." She flipped through the plastic baggies, her nerves almost choking her. "Here they are."

She almost ripped the bag out of the plastic sleeve as she shook a couple of yellow antibiotic pills into her hand. "You need to take these, and I need to examine this leg."

He didn't look happy, but he swallowed the pills. At least she hoped he did. He could be holding them under his tongue for all she knew.

"Come on," she said, standing up and moving to the back wall again. She zipped up her pack and piled the emergency blanket on it. "You're sitting back here while I look at that leg. I'm going to do whatever I need to do to save it."

"Save it?" His voice pitched up a little.

"That got your attention, didn't it?" She squatted and looped her arm under his and around his shoulders. Wow, he was strong and broad, and the only way she got them both standing was because he did most of the work with his left leg.

With a grunt, she turned and helped him to the makeshift soft spot in the cave, where he almost collapsed again. Out of breath now, she tried not to think that they'd only moved ten feet. If it came to her having to help him down the trail? She could never do that.

Pushing the thoughts away, she turned her attention back to his leg. "I haven't been in nursing school for a long time," she said. "But I think I remember a few things."

"I didn't realize you never finished," he said.

She looked at him, but it was hard to see his eyes with

the flashlight so close to her face. "It got to be too much." That was all she could say. Orchid's husband had died, and Eden didn't want to keep working all day and going to school at night. Her sister needed her help, and she'd given up her education in favor of a second job at night.

In fact, that was how she'd met Holden in the first place. She'd always told him she was going to go back, and she did for one semester. In the end, though, she'd decided she didn't want to be a nurse.

Couldn't stand to see people in pain and not be able to do anything about it.

Exactly like Holden on this mountain.

She drew in a deep breath. "I went back a couple of weeks before we broke up." She touched the outer rim of the red area, and she could feel a distinct difference between his uninfected skin and the injured area. "It wasn't the same. A lot of work, and it's not like I didn't want to work. I'm fine with working."

"You're a hard worker," Holden agreed.

She tapped on his skin, probably a little too hard, but she wanted to see how squishy the area was. He hissed and said, "Ouch, Eden, ow, ow, ow." He sucked in a breath and pressed it out between tight lips once, and then again.

"Sorry," she murmured. The skin looked angry and bright red, and she didn't see any white areas that indicated pus. She couldn't just cut into his leg. Could she? She glanced at him, wondering if he'd even know.

In the end, she decided to rely on the power of the

antibiotics and check his wound again when it wasn't pitch black. She wanted to see the skin and leg in regular light, not this weak, flickering flashlight light that was more yellow than anything.

"You're taking more antibiotics in a few hours," she said, folding the flaps of his pantleg over his leg again.

"I'm sure I'll be fine."

"The only thing you should be sure of, Holden, is that you're not getting off this mountain without help."

He sighed and looked away, which Eden took as the perfect time to plunge them back into blackness.

A few beats of silence passed, and then he asked, "How's Orchid these days?"

"Good," she said, scooting back until she leaned against the wall too, right beside him. "With the right counseling, she's been doing really well."

"I'm glad."

"So you and Dean are still best friends," she said, not really asking.

"Yeah," Holden said with a chuckle. "Though I'm considering trading him out for someone else."

"Why's that?"

"He keeps trying to set me up with someone."

Eden couldn't help the splash of laughter that filled the cave. She clapped a hand over her mouth. "I'm sorry," she said, still giggling. "That just sounded so funny."

Thankfully, Holden chuckled too. His hand slid

down her arm, and his fingers threaded right between hers. Easily, the way they always had.

She sobered instantly, her heart now booming so loudly in her chest she was sure Holden could hear it. She could almost feel the weight of his eyes as he searched the darkness for hers, and she closed her eyes and just breathed.

"So you're not interested in dating?" she asked, her voice much too high to play off as casual.

"Depends," he said, his voice throaty and low.

Eden didn't know what else to say, and thankfully, Holden said, "I feel woozy and weird."

"Probably all the water, mixed with the pills," she said. "Try to go to sleep." She hoped and prayed he wouldn't throw up. In their cramped space and with the limited sight, she didn't need to navigate around that.

He groaned, and she shifted so he could lean into her more. "Come on," she said, removing her hand from his so she could lift her arm over his shoulders. "Lie down more. It's okay. Lean into me."

"I'm sorry," he slurred.

"It's not your fault," she said, reaching over to stroke his hair off his forehead. Holden had always had amazing hair, and she worked the dirt out of the front part of it as his breathing deepened.

"I miss you," she whispered into the resulting silence, and then she closed her eyes too. Sleep took a long time to claim her, as her mind felt like it had been lit up with a dozen light bulbs.

But eventually, the warmth of Holden's body against hers lulled her back toward unconsciousness.

She didn't dare go all the way under, in case he woke again and needed something. The heat of his body concerned her, and she thought through her nursing education, trying to find the solution to his health problems.

No matter what, when she got back to her house, she was stocking her hiking backpack with more food, more medicine, more of everything.

CHAPTER SIX

a fire raged through Holden's body, consuming his flesh and making him sweat. He crawled toward the open rectangle of light ahead, because surely it would be cool there. The blue sky called to him, and though his throat felt like he'd swallowed half of the ocean's sand, he continued forward.

There'd be water in the blue sky doorway too. He just knew it.

"Holden," a woman said, and he imagined her to be wearing a beautiful, flowing, violet dress. "Wake up."

She didn't sound very nice, and Holden flinched away from the voice.

"Holden." Something wet and cool touched his face, and his eyes opened, the rectangle disappearing. "Wake up, Holden." A sob filled his ears, and everything rushed forward.

"Eden?" His voice sounded rusty, and his throat felt like fire.

"Holden." Relief filled her voice, and she came into his line of sight. "I have a little more water here. You need to drink, and you need to take more meds."

"I can't," he said, lifting his hand to wave her away. He just needed to get to that blue sky.

She touched his forehead again with a wet cloth, and he realized she'd sacrificed some of their water to make a cold compress. "You're on fire," she said. "Swallow these now."

Holden did what she said, because he was tired of arguing. Tired of being in this cave. Tired of fighting with his shareholder board about company policies and payroll and what direction they should take next. Tired of so many things.

He opened his eyes again, his mind a little clearer. "We're stuck in a cave."

"Yes," she said. "Sort of. It's only closed here at the back. It's not a real cave."

Sunlight beckoned to him, just like in the dream. "Is someone coming? Have you talked to anyone today?" He pushed himself to a sitting position and recognized the pins and needles in his back and legs. "I need to get up."

"I don't think so."

"Everything is falling asleep," he said, looking at Eden. The sunlight illuminated her, showing him all the dirt on her face and in her hair. But she was absolutely beautiful to him. He reached out and touched her face, cupping her cheek in his palm. "Please help me get up. I just need to take a few steps. Or even just lean against the wall for a minute."

Already his breath was coming quicker, but he sucked in and held all the air in his lungs while Eden positioned herself to help him stand up. Together, they achieved the feat, and he put his weight on his left leg and leaned against the wall beside him.

The blood started flowing through his body better, and sweet relief entered his mind and body. "Those pills work fast," he said.

"I couldn't wake you up," she said. "You have an infection raging through your body. We need to do something about it really soon, or you could lose your leg."

Holden looked down at his leg. "All right. What do we need to do then?" He noticed she hadn't answered him about if she'd gotten ahold of someone or not.

"I think I should just…lance it."

Holden reached up to the cut on his forehead, and his skin felt hot to his own touch. "Okay," he said. "Let's do it."

"Are you sure?"

He met her eye, wishing things between them had ended differently last time. Could he tell her that? She'd let him hold her hand last night, and then he'd settled into her embrace to sleep.

That's because she's worried about you, he told himself.

"I trust you," he said, and the hard lines in her face softened. She bent to get something out of her pack, and she smartly didn't show it to him.

She knelt in front of him with the words, "Don't kick me," and tucked his ripped pantleg out of the way.

His stomach writhed, as he'd swallowed all those pills without eating. But he wasn't going to ask her for more of her food. He'd already taken so much from her. Now, and five years ago.

He pressed his eyes closed and tried to grip the rock beside him. Because this was going to hurt. Everything in him felt strung tight, and Eden still didn't touch him. Just when he felt like he was about to snap, more pain than he'd ever experienced shot through his whole body.

He cried out against his will, and Eden put pressure on his leg. "I'm sorry," she said, her voice too high. "I'm sorry. Sorry, sorry, sorry."

Holden grunted and groaned, needing to get away from the pain. But it radiated everywhere, and he did have to work hard not to kick her.

"I've got it," she said. "I'm sorry, just a little bit more. It's coming out. There's definite infection here, but it's draining. I've got it, Holden. This is good." She kept talking, telling him about some training she did years ago.

He knew she was trying to distract him, but it wasn't really working. The pain settled to a dull ache, and for a minute he thought he was actually feeling better. That was probably because when she'd stabbed him, it had hurt so dang bad.

"I've got it all," she said. "I hope. I'm bandaging it now. We'll keep an eye on your fever and hopefully you'll start to feel better quickly."

"So someone's not coming today," he said, opening his eyes and looking down at her. She spun in his vision until he blinked her into one single person.

"Iris said the landslide covered the road. They're working on clearing it, but it probably won't be until tomorrow."

Holden didn't want to say anything, but he felt like he had to. "We need more food."

"I'll see what I can find."

"On our slab of rock?" Holden didn't mean to bite out the words, but he was tired, and hungry, and in a lot of pain. And who knew what his shareholders would do without him there? He didn't even want to think about it.

"Yes, Holden," she said acidly. "On our slab of rock." She straightened, and she looked tired and hungry and like she'd been crying.

"I'm—"

She spun and marched out of the cave before he could finish the apology. He said, "Sorry," anyway, wishing he could go after her. Honestly, he was worried the outside ledge wouldn't hold his weight combined with hers, and he had to admit he couldn't really walk anywhere on his own.

He couldn't stay in the half-cave for another minute, so he limped his way out into the fresh air. Instantly, everything was better. Sunlight. Blue sky. He breathed, for maybe the first time since the landslide.

Hawaii had fruit trees growing everywhere. Surely he and Eden could find something to eat. Thinking of Eden, he glanced around for her, and she stood way over by the edge, facing the ocean.

Even though he couldn't see her face, he sensed a vulnerability in her, and he hated that he'd snapped at her. He stepped over to her, the ground steady and secure. "I'm sorry, Eden," he said.

"You need to eat."

He couldn't disagree, but he didn't know what to do about it. "My leg feels better," he said. "And I'm pretty sure I passed some fruit trees on the way up."

She looked at him, her oceanic eyes searching his. "And how do you plan to get across that gap?" She nodded to it. "Because if we can do that, we can get down. We don't need fruit."

"What about up then?" he asked, turning back to the cave area. He walked that way, taking short then big steps, a strange sort of gait. He glanced down at the pile of debris from the path above, but he edged past it and the rock overhang where he'd hid from the rain.

Sure enough, the path continued even if it was a bit

muddy and littered with branches and rocks. "We can keep going up," he called to Eden.

She joined him, her worry like waves in the atmosphere. "What if there's no shelter further up?"

"Do you think it will rain?"

"It better," she said, glancing up into the cloudless sky. "We don't have any drinking water. Well, we have a few swallows left, but no way to cap it."

She didn't say he'd lost the bottle, but he heard it in her words anyway. "I think we go up," he said. "You've been up here, right? Isn't there a spring?"

"That's *miles* up there," she said. "Like, almost to the top."

"Let's go, then."

"Holden, you can barely walk."

He looked at her, his desire to do what she wanted and make her happy warring with his hunger and thirst. "Eden, we can't stay here. I know they say to find a safe spot and stay there until you're found, but we're not really lost. They just can't get to us. And we have to eat and drink." Holden faced the path he'd been walking yesterday when the mountain had fallen. "I don't think we have a choice. There's no food and no water here."

He touched her arm. "I'll be slow, but you can go ahead of me." Her eyes locked onto his, and he saw the worry there. "I can do this."

Eden's eyes closed in a slow blink, and she tipped

up to kiss him on the cheek. "I know you can. Let me get the backpack."

Holden watched her duck back into the cave area, the spot where her lips had touched burning hotter with every passing moment.

Eden returned, her backpack in place. "Okay. Ready?"

"Yes," he said.

"If you need to stop, say something. If something hurts, say something. If—"

"Eden," he said. "Everything hurts. I promise you I'll let you know if I need to take a break." He swept his eyes down her body. "I can't believe you're not more hurt."

"My back hurts," she admitted. "And my elbow." She glanced down at her feet. "And my ankle."

For some reason, this made Holden feel better. At least he wasn't the only broken one. "So we'll both go slow and say when we need a break."

"Deal." She smiled at him, and Holden couldn't remember the last time that had happened. His heart skipped around inside his chest, and he let Eden go ahead of him. He glanced at his watch, surprised to see it was just after nine o'clock in the morning. He hadn't realized he'd slept so late, and he thought his fever had kept him down longer than he'd intended.

The meeting had probably started a few minutes ago too, and he thought of Joan, the eagle-eyed woman who seemed to disagree with everything he'd done since taking over the company after his mother's death.

But his idea of what Explore Getaway Bay should do was completely different than Joan's. She only cared about money, and he cared about the service, the employees, and the product they were putting out.

If that cost him a few more dollars, so be it. He had plenty.

He stepped as quickly as he could, but he gave up worrying if he was holding Eden back or not. She went at her speed, stopping to wait for him on her own timetable. When he wanted to stop, he did. His tongue felt like a sponge in his mouth, and he told himself they'd reach the top eventually.

They'd been walking for an hour and a half when Eden yelled, "Holden!" with pure excitement in her voice. He looked up from the ground, where he'd been keeping his attention during the climb.

He couldn't see her up ahead, so he called, "What?" and kept walking. Glance down, step. Glance up. He'd only taken a few steps this way when Eden appeared, waving both of her hands above her head.

"Sea grapes and bananas!" She ran back toward him, and he noticed her limping too. But her excitement and the prospect of food had him moving faster than normal.

Eden reached him and handed him a short, stubby banana, very unlike the ones he bought in the grocery store, but exactly like a wild banana should be. "Come on," she said. "There's lots more, and I think I saw a mango tree too."

Her eyes shone with excitement, and for the first time since the landslide, Holden actually thought he could have a second chance with the woman who'd never truly given him back his heart.

CHAPTER SEVEN

*E*den knew she should eat slower, but she couldn't seem to get her mouth to obey her brain. That happened a lot, honestly, and her mouth sometimes got her in trouble. But beside her, Holden was eating through his seventh piece of fruit, with the pile in front of them getting smaller every minute.

Food.

They had food.

Yes, they still needed water, but Eden estimated they probably had another three or four hours to the spring. The rate they climbed certainly wasn't fast, but she could do it. She could get water and bring it back to him if she had to.

The weather was playing nice—or nasty. She couldn't decide. Depending on how she looked at it determined how she felt. She'd love to be able to just collect rainwater, but that meant staying down in the cave instead of eating up here in the wild fruit trees.

There had been a mango tree, and she'd managed to knock down eight of them. She put the last sea grape she could possibly eat in her mouth, spit out the stone, and sighed as she leaned against the tree trunk.

"So now we won't die," she said. Sure, they might run into a feral pig or goat, but it wasn't like Getaway Bay played home to cougars or lions. Their biggest danger remained Holden's leg, and she glanced down to his calf. "How's your leg?"

"It feels okay, actually," he said, looking at her as he licked mango juice from his fingers.

Eden's whole body turned blazing hot, as if someone had poured gasoline down her throat and tossed a match in afterward.

Probably because she knew what it felt like to be kissed with that mouth. She tore her eyes from him and looked out into the wilderness. They'd moved around the mountain now, so the ocean sat behind them, but the view before her was still spectacular. If she looked carefully enough, she could see the black ribbon of highway that came around from the cattle ranch.

"Do you miss the ranch?" she asked, suddenly nostalgic for the time she'd spent there with him.

"A little," he said, which in Holden-speak really meant a lot.

"Your dad must've given it to Lincoln."

"He did, yes," he said. "I got some percentage of his wealth in a buy-out."

Eden nodded though she was a bit surprised. Holden and his father hadn't gotten along back when she'd last dated him.

"He did it out of loyalty to my mother, if you can believe that."

"I don't know what to believe," Eden said, cutting a look at him out of the corner of her eye. She didn't know his father personally. Only what Holden had told her, and she knew he carried emotional trauma from feelings of abandonment. She knew he'd protected his mother fiercely, and she'd always liked that about Holden.

His intensity was as attractive to her as it was maddening at times.

"What did you do with the money?" she asked.

"Buried my mother," he said. His daggered glance meant that conversation was over, and Eden could admit she probably shouldn't have asked. Holden had always hated that his half-brother had more than him—more time with his dad. More duties on the ranch. More money.

"Well, I make twenty bucks an hour taking people on tours around the island," she said. "So I'm sure you're doing better than me."

"Does it matter if I am?"

"Not to me."

"You really only make twenty bucks an hour?" The interest in his voice caused her to look at him again.

"Yeah," she said. "Explore Getaway Bay pays the best out of the tour companies. I mean, besides the helicopter tours or the whale watching or the parasailing. But I can't fly a helicopter or pilot a speedboat. So...yeah." She shrugged. "It's a good job. I like it."

"That's good to know," he said, and she cocked her head.

"Good to know?"

"Echo that," he said, standing up by leaning into the tree and using it to hold his weight.

"Echo what?" She had no idea what he was talking about.

He chuckled and shook his head, wiping his hands through his dirty hair. He really was sexy while muddy, and she tried not to think about him like that. Or think about how she must look.

"It's programmer speak," he said. "Never mind." He glanced at his watch. "I think we should get going. How long to the spring, do you think?"

"A few more hours," she said vaguely. "I want you to take more pills."

"Drug me up, beautiful," he said, and she could've sworn he was flirting with her. The sly smile. The sparkling eyes. And that nickname. She'd never felt particularly beautiful. Eden didn't care about makeup or hair products. She didn't wear heels or strappy sundresses to the beach. She only went to the beach if

64

she heard there were turtles there or she could collect seashells.

But for those six months while she'd dated Holden, when he called her beautiful, she believed him.

And she did now too.

To hide her blush, she bent over her backpack to find the painkillers and the antibiotics. He swallowed both dry while she loaded the leftover fruit into her backpack. "I'm just going to gather enough for tonight too," she told him. "Just in case there's nothing up there."

And there likely wouldn't be. From her rusty recollection, the spring sat just above the tree line, and that meant nothing grew up there.

Holden helped pull down mangoes, and they filled her backpack with everything it would hold. Way more than dinner and breakfast, but neither of them said that.

Eden wanted to keep thinking positively. Keep hoping that the road could be cleared, and the rescue teams could get up the mountain to them that day. She wondered what her mother was thinking, and if anyone at work missed her.

Cotton, probably. A fellow tour guide, he was close to her age, and he constantly encouraged Eden in her outdoor survival inventions. She'd only gone on her last two appointments with those finnicky billionaires because of him. She'd told him about all the failures too, and he just kept telling her not to give up.

Anna too. She booked all the large group tours, and she often assigned them to Eden, because she was "the best." They talked about the men Anna dated, and Eden's dating disasters. Yes, Anna would definitely be worried about Eden.

Don't give up, Cotton would tell her.

You'll meet right man, Anna had often said.

As Eden adjusted the straps on her backpack, she watched Holden get a head start on the hike. She wasn't going to give up out here. She was a survivor, and she'd make it through this.

"Maybe I've already met the right man," she whispered to herself, Holden's broad shoulders just as powerful now as they'd been five years ago. And maybe she shouldn't give up on him either.

Her friends continued to bicker silently in her mind, but Eden focused on the path in front of her. Her injuries weren't nearly as bad as Holden's, but she knew her ankle wasn't at one-hundred percent, and the last thing they needed was for both of them to be immobile.

"You're doing awesome," she said, catching up to Holden easily despite her wounds. "Can I walk with you for a while?"

"Of course," he said with a smile, this one not nearly as flirtatious. Which totally meant he'd been flirting with her earlier. Eden almost couldn't believe it. A warm feeling spread through her, and she hiked slowly next to him.

"I think if I had a walking stick, I could go faster," he said. "Do you think we might be able to find something?"

"That's a great idea," she said. "We should've broken off one of the branches on that big tree we ate by." She turned around and glanced behind her. It felt like their lunch spot was so far away.

"Too thick," he said. "And we don't have anything to cut it."

"I do," she said. "If you held the branch down for me, I could do it. I'll cut off the tip so it's not so thick."

"You really want to go back?"

No, she didn't. But they'd only been walking at Holden's speed for maybe five minutes. "Let's do it," she said, and she started down the path ahead of him. By the time he got there, she had all the fruit unpacked, the cord out, and her knife ready.

"What is that?" he asked when he saw her tool.

"I made it," she said. "It's a way better all-in-one tool, and it has a serrated edge. See?" She showed him, trusting that he wouldn't laugh at her or say something else had already been made and it worked "well enough."

Eden didn't want well enough. None of the products on the market right now had serrated knives, and she'd be hacking at this tree branch forever if she had to use a straight edge.

"That's great, Eden," he said, a measure of awe in his voice. "So this and the can cooker. What else have you got?" He seemed genuinely interested, but some of Eden's defenses flew into place anyway.

"I have a few things," she said, not wanting to tell him that she spent all her spare time either on bad first dates or in her shed, making outdoor survival products no one wanted. She moved around the tree, looking at the branches. "This one looks good." She glanced at him. "You hold it down, okay? Tell me if you need to let it go."

"I got it," he said, moving into position. He bent the tree limb over, stutter-stepping with it until she could reach it. She made quick, tight sawing motions with the knife, actually surprised at how quickly it moved through the wood.

"Got it," she said, and he moved backward through the motions of letting the limb back up. She switched to the straight blade now, and quickly got rid of any extraneous branches and leaves before setting the walking stick on the ground beside her.

"Seems tall enough," she said, moving over to him and handing him the stick. "What do you think?"

He positioned it on his right side and leaned into it to step. "I think I'm going to be able to go about ten times faster." He beamed at her, and added, "Thank you, Eden."

"It was your idea, Holden." She didn't need to take credit for having a knife in her pack, even if it was a superior product than what currently existed.

"You should sell your inventions," he said as they

started up the path again. He did move a lot faster, and Eden liked that they'd be able to hike beside one another instead of her so far ahead.

She snorted. "You're joking, right?"

"Why would I be joking? That was awesome. It had cord in it and everything."

"Well, I'm afraid you're the only one who thinks it was awesome," she said. "I've been around to probably a dozen investors—or guys who claim to be investors. They have the right number of zeroes in their bank accounts to be investors. None of them wanted anything I have."

She heard the bitterness in her own voice. "Maybe I should talk to Lincoln. Now that he's a cattle rancher billionaire, maybe he'd invest in my survival products." She laughed, not really thinking she'd ask Lincoln.

She was done with that. She couldn't handle another meeting. Getting her hopes up only to have them dashed again.

Nope.

She'd take Holden's compliments, but she wasn't going to waste her time on lost causes anymore.

Her mind needled her with one last question: *Is Holden a lost cause?*

CHAPTER EIGHT

*H*olden kept his mouth shut, though he wanted to shout that he could be her billionaire investor. He had the right number of zeroes in his bank account, mostly from his wealth in Explore Getaway Bay, but his inheritance in the cattle ranch had put him into the ten-figure category.

He'd recently been contacted by a man named Fisher DuPont, the owner of Sweet Breeze Resort and Spa. Apparently, they had some sort of Nine-0 Club he wanted Holden to join. Holden hadn't found the time to meet with the man, though he was a friend of Theo's.

All at once, he realized that Theo was most likely in the club already.

"I even met with your boss," Eden said, drawing Holden back to the conversation. "He wasn't interested."

"Well, Theo does technology," he said. "I'm going to —" He cut off before he could utter the next word. That was the second time he'd almost slipped enough to let her know he was more than just a computer scientist for The Web Developer.

When she'd said his company paid the best, he'd been pleased—and he'd almost given away too much. Eden had a way of making him say things he wouldn't normally say. He liked it as much as he didn't.

"You're going to what?" she asked.

He cleared his throat, and he wondered if she recognized the sign of a lie. She'd always known his tells in the past. But she just kept stepping with him, each of them slowly making their way up the mountain.

"I'm going to be working on an app for Explore Getaway Bay." He glanced at her and looked back at the ground. She watched it too, and he wished he'd suggested she cut her own walking stick as her limp remained.

She didn't need to know he'd *hired* Theo do develop the app. Well, Dean had. And then he'd asked Theo to make sure Holden got the project for his "enthusiasm for the outdoors."

It had landed on his desk just last week. He hadn't started yet, but he found it ironic to be getting paid to develop an app he was also paying to have developed. He smiled just thinking about it.

"That's great," she said. "Tourists love apps."

"They do," he said. "What would you have on the app? From a tour guide perspective."

"Oh, I don't know," she said. "I'm not great with apps myself."

"Would you use one as an employee?" he asked anyway. "Like if you could see your schedule or text in to say you were sick or report a problem with a guest. Something like that."

"Yeah, that would probably be great," she said. "Would anyone lose their job?"

"Why would someone lose their job?"

"Like my friend Anna. She schedules all the large groups. If they did that on the app, would Anna still have a job?"

"Of course," he said. "She'd still have to contact them. Find out their needs. Schedule the guide and the vehicles. All of that. Basically the booking comes in as an email to Anna, instead of a phone call."

"That's pretty cool," she said. "I think that would be great. And if I could see my paycheck, or what I've been booked to do right on my phone, any time, that would be great too."

"If someone texts in sick, those shifts or tours or whatever would come up, and others could claim them," he said. "There are a lot of cool options."

"Sounds like it."

Holden wished he didn't have to focus so much on walking. Then maybe he'd be able to hold her hand while they walked, pretend that they were on a romantic walk through the wilderness instead of a march for their lives.

They walked in silence for a while, until she finally asked, "Do you think your co-workers are worried about you?"

"Yes," he said, thinking of the state Dean would be in by now. "Dean probably has us on the news stations and everything."

"Really?"

"He's a bit high-strung."

Eden giggled, immediately covering her mouth with her hand. "Sorry," she said with sparkling eyes.

"It's fine," Holden said, laughing too. "I said it, and it's true."

"That must be why you guys get along so great," she said. "You're *so* laid back and he worries about enough for the both of you."

"That's about it," Holden said, thinking she'd nailed his friendship with Dean pretty well. "You think I'm laid back? After I basically broke down when my mother died?" He'd only talked about his feelings during that dark time with his grief counselor, but he found he wanted to clear the air with Eden.

"I mean, yeah," she said, her ponytail falling between them. "That was just an isolated incident. You…reacted the way you did because you feel intensely, not because you're high-strung or intense in personality."

Holden let her words sink through him, trying to

make them align in his mind. "I feel intensely," he repeated slowly.

"Yeah," she said. "Don't you think?" She paused and looked at him. "I need to take a break."

"Yeah, okay." Holden wiped his hand across his sweaty forehead. "Me too." He sure would like a drink, but he accepted another mango from Eden as she took one out of her backpack for herself. His stomach ached quietly, probably from all the fruit and all the pills, but he said nothing as he peeled back the rind to get to the juice inside.

"I hope I didn't offend you when I said you feel intensely," Eden said after they'd rested for a few minutes.

"No," he said. "You didn't."

"You just never responded."

"I guess I was just thinking," he said. "I mean, it's true. I was devastated when my mom died. It broke me." He couldn't look at her. "And when we were together, it was some of the happiest times of my life." He'd loved her deeply, even if he'd never said those three words out loud to her. "Honestly, it was like I was on a roller coaster during those six months."

"I know," she said, and he looked at her to see if there was any sarcasm there. Didn't seem to be, and he reached over and took her hand in his.

"I still...feel intensely about you, Eden," he said, wondering if he'd just blown everything wide open.

Her eyes definitely widened, and she slipped her

hand out from under his. "I'm sure you'll feel differently once we get back to civilization."

He didn't think so, and he opened his mouth to argue.

"Please don't say anything else," she said, a blip of rare emotion entering her voice. Eden was so tough on the outside, and so tender inside. Holden had seen both sides of her when she'd trusted him enough to open up. He wanted that again.

"Why not?" he asked, realizing that if he did pursue a relationship with her, she'd have to be privy to certain information—including what company he owned and how much money he had in his bank account.

But his heart didn't seem to care about those secrets. His heart wanted her back in his life. His heart wanted a woman to care about—and it wanted Eden.

"I don't know," she said. "I just...it took me a very long time to get over you, Holden. I don't think I could survive falling for you again, only to have my heart broken twice." She started up the path again, but Holden didn't even have his walking stick in his hand.

He grabbed it from where he'd leaned it against a rock, but he couldn't move. "Falling for me...*again*?"

Had she been in love with him too? How had he not known?

"You didn't even know your own name back then," he muttered, checking the ground before stepping. His leg felt loads better, and he managed to catch up to her several minutes later, when she paused at the top of the next rise.

"I'm sorry," he said to her, hoping it covered all the bases for things he needed to apologize for. "I didn't know I'd hurt you so much last time."

She looked at him, her eyes so clear and still calling to him in a way only Eden McLaughlin ever had. "I know that, Holden. Like I said, you feel intensely. The good and the bad." She patted him on the shoulder like he was her brother and started up the path again.

"I want it to be good," he said after her, and thankfully, she turned back. "Between us," he added, his throat so dry. "I—I want us to be okay. To be friends."

His heart wailed at the word *friends*, but his mouth had already spoken it.

"We are friends, Holden."

"So if I were up here alone, and you saw my face on the news, would you be worried?" He took the few steps between them and stood in front of her, the memory of her lips on his cheek just that morning still fresh.

"Yes."

He studied her for a few moments, probably too many. "I'd be worried about you too, Eden."

———

HOURS LATER, HOLDEN HADN'T SAID anything else to embarrass himself, and they'd reached the spring. Pure relief flowed through him at the trickle of water coming out of the rocks only fifteen feet above the tree line.

His whole body ached despite the medicine he'd taken that day, and he cupped his hands to catch the water, drinking and drinking and not feeling satisfied.

He finally stopped when Eden made him. "We don't have to drink it all right now," she said, a teasing quality in her voice he liked. "It'll be dark soon, and we need to figure out shelter."

There were plenty of rocks up here, but the wind was going to be their biggest opponent now. "It'll be easy to go down into the trees," he said. "And back up here for something to drink."

"Not if you do it in the middle of the night," she said, turning toward him. "Let's just make that a rule. Rule number one. Do not go wandering in the night, even if you're thirsty."

"I walked all the way up here," Holden said, taking a few steps toward her. "I can walk to get a drink."

"The edge is only a few feet from here," she said. "Please? Can't that be the rule? If I need a drink, I'll wake you up. If you need one, you wake me up."

"All right," he said, deciding to employ the laid back side of himself instead of the fired up side. "Can I go to the bathroom alone?" he muttered as she walked away.

"Only if you don't fall off the cliff to do it," she tossed over her shoulder. In the next moment, she laughed, and Holden couldn't help joining her.

They went back down the path and off the path into the trees. There were big boulders here too, and a couple of them together made a nice little room with walls on two sides. A grouping of eucalyptus trees provided some good cover for them, and it was almost like a spot had been made for them.

"What about here?" he asked, noting the ground was flat and relatively smooth. "I can gather leaves for a ground covering, and it'll provide some shelter from the wind up here."

There were a few banyan trees up this high, but the leaves weren't nearly what they were down at the lower elevations, with waterfalls nearby. But it would be better than sleeping on rocks. Eden agreed to the spot by setting her backpack down beside the boulder, and the two of them got to work gathering whatever they thought they needed to make it through the night.

She removed all the fruit from her pack and began stuffing it with eucalyptus and other types of leaves. "A pillow," she pronounced, obviously quite proud of herself.

Holden couldn't help smiling at her, though she'd basically rejected his idea of starting a relationship. But he couldn't let go of the idea of a second chance romance with her.

People got second chances. Maybe this time he wouldn't be so consumed with feelings of loss and dealing with familial matters that he'd lose her.

Maybe this time, they could make it work.

His hopes lifted and kept him working long past the time when his body was crying to him to stop.

Finally, with his bed made out of leaves and using her zipper bag as a leaf-filled pillow, he collapsed in the V of the two boulders with the words, "I'm exhausted."

"Me too," Eden said, pulling her much bigger and softer pillow over to his left side. She sighed as she leaned into him and allowed him to drape his arm around her shoulders. "Me too."

CHAPTER NINE

*E*den was just starting to fall asleep when Holden asked, "What are you doing?"

She'd have to be deaf not to hear the growly undertone in his voice. "Sleeping."

"I'm confused. I told you I still had feelings for you, and you shut me down. Fast," he said, his breath wafting over her shoulder. "And now you're all cuddled into me."

Eden straightened, but she was immediately cold. The higher elevations in Hawaii could be chilly, and they were at the highest one on the island of Getaway Bay.

"I just thought...." Her voice trailed off, and she searched his face in the gathering darkness. He had a tremendous ability to hide how he felt until it exploded out of him, and right now, he wore a stoic mask.

"What did you think, Eden?" He remained very still, and Eden wasn't entirely sure what she was thinking.

I still feel intensely about you, Eden.

The words in his husky voice hadn't left her mind since he'd said them.

"Look, it's just cold up here, and I was hoping we could share the heat source." She looked pointedly at him. "That's you, by the way. You never get cold."

A lazy smile crossed his face, and Eden really liked it. Felt one stretching her lips too.

No, she commanded herself. Just because she was attracted to him didn't mean they could have a relationship. She'd been kicking herself for kissing his cheek that morning for the entire day.

"Tell me why you think my feelings for you would change just because we get back to town."

Eden blinked at him. "You haven't been interested for five years, Holden. *Five years.* And I'm supposed to believe that just because we get stuck together for a few days, you're magically interested in me again?"

Holden gazed evenly back at her. "Yes."

Eden opened her mouth to argue and found she had none. "I—"

"Has it ever occurred to you that perhaps I'm embarrassed about how things ended between us last time?"

Eden didn't know surprise could layer on top of itself the way it was. "Things ended fine, Holden," she said. "I don't hold any grudges against you."

"That's obviously not true."

A gust of wind blasted right into their makeshift shelter, and Eden shivered. Holden lifted his arm, and she hesitated for only a moment before slipping back into his embrace. He really was a human heater, and she sighed as her body absorbed the warmth from his.

"I really don't feel badly about how we ended." It was much easier to talk to him when she didn't have to look into those dark as night eyes. And she didn't harbor ill feelings toward him for how they'd ended, only that they'd ended at all.

"Well, I do," he said. "And I'd really like to take you to dinner when we get back to town. No fruit. Nothing with mango or banana, I promise."

She laughed quietly, and Holden did too, a delicious secret between them now.

"What do you think?" he asked.

Eden thought she'd get her heart filleted again. "I think dinner would be nice."

"Are you serious?"

"You don't have to sound so shocked."

"I think I'm entitled," he said. "I mean, after what you said—"

"I know what I said," Eden snapped. "Maybe I'm just starving and anything besides mango sounds good. Have you thought of that?"

"Mm." He pulled her closer and slid his lips along her hairline. And Eden finally slept.

When she woke, the first rays of light had barely

started to brighten the day. Only the second day in the mountains, but it felt like she'd been up here with Holden for weeks.

"Morning," he said softly.

"You must be feeling better." Yesterday, she hadn't even been able to wake him. The terror that had flowed through her veins felt as real now as it had then.

"A lot better," he said. "Still sore from sleeping on the ground, but my leg barely hurts."

"Want me to look at it?" she asked.

"Yeah, check it out and see if it's better."

Eden looked at his leg, and it was hardly red at all. "It looks great, Holden." She smiled up at him. "And we have enough fruit for breakfast. And water just up the hill."

They'd survived the rain. The wind last night. The challenge of finding food and water.

Now their biggest obstacle would be boredom.

Eden kept herself busy for about half an hour as she ate and walked up the trail to get a drink. She excused herself to use the woods as a bathroom, and she stayed out in the trees for a few extra minutes, staring up into the sky and wondering why she'd accepted an invitation to dinner with her ex-boyfriend.

She didn't feel crazy, but she was certainly acting like it. Maybe desperate times called for desperate measures. She'd been cold. He was warm. Maybe she'd said what he wanted to hear, but she didn't think so.

If Anna were here, she'd tell Eden to jump at the

chance to go out with Holden, and Eden actually felt like leaping.

When she got back to their tree branch shelter, Holden wasn't there but several more pieces of fruit sat on the leaves. She sat down and pulled all the leaves out of her backpack. She didn't have cards or puzzles or anything to pass the time. Just her own thoughts, and she didn't want to spend much time there.

"I found a new kind of fruit," Holden said, walking toward her. He still leaned heavily on the walking stick, but he carried a few pieces of papaya and laid them down before sitting beside her.

"Does your phone have power? Can we call and let someone know where we are?"

Eden pulled the phone out of the front pocket of the backpack. "I doubt there will be any service up here," she said. "I think there are new cell phone towers coming in, because Getaway Bay is growing so much, but I don't think they're here yet."

She powered on her phone, and sure enough, there was no service. Not even a fraction of one little bar. She tilted the phone toward him. "See?"

"Should we go back down?" he asked. "As soon as we see we have a signal, we send a message. Say we're up at the spring."

"I guess we could," she said, but her ankle and the whole rest of her body did not like that idea. "We probably should've left a note or something."

"Do you have paper in your magic backpack?"

Eden laughed, wishing she had a way to wash her hair up here. Maybe she could at least hold her hair under the spring, even if she didn't have shampoo and conditioner. "If my backpack were magical, I would've pulled out a jet pack and gotten us off this mountain."

"Wow." Holden chuckled most of the word out. "A jet pack."

"What would you want in a magical backpack?" she asked, enjoying this game a little too much. Or maybe just enough. Maybe this would be her and Holden's new way of being. Would they hike back up to this spring every spring to remember how they'd met?

"Oh, I don't know," he said. "Toilet paper, for one. One of those machines that replicates food from Star Trek."

Eden giggled and she picked up one of the pieces of fruit he'd brought back. "And what would you have the food replicator make?"

"Pizza," he said. "All meat, with extra cheese. And some of those pork potstickers from that new place on Gardenia. Have you been there?"

"Yeah, I had one of my first dates there." Eden realized a bit too late what she'd said.

Holden didn't miss a beat when he said, "*One* of your first dates?"

Eden wanted to go back to the magic backpack game. Instead, she decided to be honest with him. "I've been out with several people in the last few months."

"The same guy?"

"You think I'm dating someone?"

"I don't know. That's why I'm asking."

"Holden," she said, in that same reprimanding voice she'd used when he wouldn't take the painkillers. "I told you I'd go out with you last night."

"I know." He reached over and trailed his fingers down the side of her face. "Are you seeing someone else?"

"No," she said. "I've had a string of first dates. Can't get a second." She gazed evenly at him, almost daring him to find anything about her love life funny.

"I'll take you on a second," he said, his dark eyes positively dreamy. If he knew he possessed eyes that drank her up and made her woozy.... *He doesn't know*, she told herself. And maybe his eyes didn't have the same effect on everyone that they had on her.

"Have you been out with anyone?" she asked.

He shook his head. "Nope."

"Not even one woman?"

"Dean's tried to set me up with people, and I've had a date or two scheduled. I always cancel at the last minute."

"Is that what you're going to do to me?"

"Nope." She smiled at her, that sweet, sly smile that said he was thinking about kissing her. In fact, his eyes dropped to her mouth, and Eden's whole soul sang.

He pushed her hair off her face, tucking the disgusting, muddy strands behind her ear. "I need to wash my hair," she whispered.

"You can do it after."

"After what?"

"After I kiss you." He leaned down, and Eden's eyelids fluttered closed, her heart skipping a beat every other pulse.

His lips brushed across hers, sending heat and fireworks through her bloodstream. She breathed in and matched his mouth to his, telling him how she felt whether she wanted to or not.

Holden Holstein might not have been out with another woman in five years, but he had not forgotten how to kiss one. How to make her feel cherished and adored. How to make her feel like he was the only man for her.

CHAPTER TEN

*H*olden couldn't believe Eden was kissing him back. She'd been so resistant to the idea of them trying again, but she certainly wasn't kissing him with any hesitation.

He'd forgotten how it felt to have every cell in his body buzzing. Every muscle sinking into a warm bath. Every stroke of his mouth against Eden's igniting the fire in his blood.

In fact, the fire inside Holden had been cold for years.

But Eden knew exactly how to stoke it, from scraping her fingernails gently along the back of his neck to sighing into his mouth as they parted.

He held her close even after their kiss ended, because he needed her strength to stand after a kiss like that. His pulse testified that he'd just run a marathon, even though he hadn't.

"Want me to help you wash your hair?" he whispered, his eyes still closed, the scent of earth laced with Eden's perfume filling his nose.

"If you want." She fell back a step, leaving Holden to balance himself on his walking stick and his good leg. "Then we can go down until we get a signal."

"Sounds like a plan."

She nodded, her eyes darting everywhere but at him, and Holden smiled to himself as she bent to get something out of her pack. She snapped an elastic ponytail holder on her wrist and reached for his hand.

Their eyes finally met, and Holden couldn't help chuckling. "You haven't been kissing any of your first dates, have you?" he asked.

"What kind of question is that?" she asked.

"Just wondering."

"I'm not easy, Holden."

Oh, that much he knew. Being with Eden had been challenging for him before, but this time, it didn't feel *hard*. She made him want to be better. Made him think about things. Opened his eyes to new possibilities.

"I was just thinking you must've been practicing that kiss," he said. "It was amazing."

Eden tripped over her own feet, and Holden's grip on her fingers tightened. Their eyes met again, and this time Eden wore a hint of embarrassment in hers. A pinkness stained her cheeks in a sexy way, and Holden couldn't help kissing her again.

"Mm," he said, pulling away before he would've liked. "Yeah. Amazing."

Eden grinned at him and said, "You're not so bad yourself. I'm not sure I believe you haven't been out with anyone since we broke up."

"Believe it," he said. "Ask Dean if you want."

"I don't need to ask Dean." They passed the tree line and came to the spring. Holden positioned himself with his bad leg against the rock while Eden crouched down and bent over to put her head in the water.

"Holy cow, that's cold," she said.

It was such a trickle that Holden had to scoop it with his hands into her hair. He ran his fingers through it, working out the worst of the dirt, mud, and grime. The action was almost erotic, the way his fingertips sizzled when they touched her scalp, despite the iciness of the water.

"I can't take anymore," she said, and Holden stepped back, completely mesmerized by her. The touch of her. The feel of her. The scent of her. The sight of her.

How had he lived this long without her in his life? Five years.

He hadn't been living at all.

She scooped her hair into a high ponytail on top of her head, squeezed the water out, and secured it with the elastic. When she faced him again, the pinkness in her cheeks had disappeared, and she looked fierce and lovely at the same time.

Holden wetted his hands and ran them through his hair a few times, feeling the mud there too. He cleaned up much quicker than she did though, and soon enough, he felt like he'd gotten all the gunk out of his hair.

"Let me get my pack," she said when they reached the spot where they detoured off the path to their shelter. When she returned, she positioned herself on his left side and slipped her hand into his.

"New game," she said, the cell phone gripped in her other hand. "You tell me something new or different about you in the past five years, and then I'll tell you something about me. Whoever can't think of something first, loses."

"You've already won," he said. "I'm the same."

"I'm sure that's not true," she said. "Number one, you have a new job."

"You said new or different," he said. "You already knew that."

"It still counts."

"All right," he said with a smile. "I have a new job at The Web Developer." *And as the owner and CEO of Explore Getaway Bay.* Why didn't he tell her that?

Maybe because she was already talking. "I got rid of my cats."

"You did?" Holden looked at her, his leg feeling better all the time. "Wow, Eden."

"My dad was allergic, and he couldn't ever come

over. So, I found a new home for them." She shrugged. "It was the right thing to do."

"Well, going off that, I got a dog."

"You did?" She sounded as surprised as he had about her losing the cats. He'd never particularly enjoyed her cats, and he couldn't say he was all that sorry about them being rehomed.

"Yeah," he said. "He's a white golden retriever. He usually comes with me when I go out hiking."

"Why didn't you bring him this time?"

"Willie's the office dog," he said. "I was only coming out for an hour or two. Just to clear my head after finishing a stressful project." He paused while she lifted the phone to check the signal.

"Nothing."

He sighed and continued with, "I'm sure Dean took him home. He sometimes does anyway."

"Willie. Nice name." She gave him a look that he couldn't interpret before he had to check the ground for his next step. "I took a pottery class."

"Yeah? You make anything?"

"One sad-looking vase," she said. "Let's just say I learned about failure during the class."

Holden chuckled. "Let's see. My turn." Again, his mind turned to Explore Getaway Bay and his role in the company. Before he could tell her he'd bought out his mother's shares in the company and become the owner because he now held seventy percent of the company in his hand, her cell phone rang.

They both froze, as if they were connected to the same rope and it had suddenly gone taut.

The phone rang again.

"Answer it," Holden said.

Eden looked at him, shock in her bright blue eyes, as she lifted the phone to her ear. "Hello?"

He couldn't hear anything, but she nodded, and he said, "You have to talk, sweetheart."

"Yes," she said, finally blinking and coming to her senses. "Yes, we're on the path that leads up to the Bald Mountain spring. We had to go all the way up for water." She glanced at him. "Yes, he's with me. Yes, just the two of us."

She turned away from him. "What do you mean? Who is this?"

Holden had the urge to grab the phone away from her, but he feared the motion would throw him off balance. So he stood there while she said, "Put a rescuer on the phone," and then, "How did you get this number?"

Holden's hopes fell with everything Eden said. They weren't any closer to getting off this mountain. It was just the press looking for a story. And he was the CEO of a survival company, caught out in the wilderness with no survival supplies.

He'd be a laughingstock on the island, and in his own company.

Dread filled his body, making his steps heavy as he started down the path without Eden. He just needed a little space. Some distance, to make his thoughts line up. She continued talking behind him, but the call ended soon after that, and she called, "Holden."

He paused and turned back toward her. She limped down to him, her face hard and angry. "That wasn't a rescuer. Some guy from The Island News, wanting to know if we were alive. Said there were rumors of three people up here, not just two."

"Just two," Holden echoed, his mind slow and thick.

"I'm going to call my sister," she said. "I only have twelve percent left on my phone." She tapped and put the phone to her ear again.

"Iris," she said, her voice filled with relief. "It's Eden. Update me. Where are the rescue crews?"

Holden didn't watch her while she spoke to her sister. He kept one ear on the conversation, but he really just looked out over the tropical beauty that was Hawaii. He'd been hiding in the shadows at Explore Getaway Bay for years. Maybe it was time to come forward, even if that painted him in a bad light for a week or two. The media would move on to some other story, and he could go back to the closed board meetings, with Dean as the public face of the company.

He could develop his app, and hold Eden's hand, kiss her goodnight and fall asleep with dreams of her in his head.

Even as he imagined the simple life, he knew it would never be his. And not just because Eden said,

"You're kidding," as more of a gasp than words. But because Holden had never had the luxury of an easy life. He'd never minded, until his mother had died. That had seemed wholly unfair, and sometimes he still wrestled with the darkness inside him.

Something pierced the air, something that didn't belong. "Do you hear that?" he asked, twisting to look over his shoulder.

Eden was off the phone, but she stood very still, her eyes pinned to him.

The noise came again. Distant, but there. High-pitched. It was a whistle.

"Someone's coming," he said. "They've made it across the gap."

"Yeah," Eden said in a voice that didn't quite belong to her. "That's what Iris just said."

"That's great. Where are they?"

"Almost here," she said as she cocked her head at the sound of the whistle. It seemed to have gotten astronomically closer in only a few seconds. "Iris said the crews worked through the night, so they could get Getaway Bay's newest billionaire back to safety." She folded her arms and glared at him.

Ice ran through his veins now, and he opened his mouth to explain.

"That's not me, so I'm assuming it must be you." She lifted her eyebrows as if to say, *Well? Is that true or not?*

"It's true," he said, answering the mental question.

"And I suppose you were just about to tell me." She started walking down the trail again, leaving him to stare after her.

"Yes," he called, getting himself moving. He felt her slipping away from him when he'd just gotten her back. "I was just about to tell you."

"Uh huh," she said. "I really believe you, Holden." She paused and spun toward him. "I can't *believe* I believed you about anything. *I still feel intensely about you, Eden.* What a joke." Her eyes flashed with that fire, and it was hot and scorching. She turned away from him and jogged a few steps.

"Eden," he said, trying to catch up to her. She was injured too, but not nearly as unstable on her feet as he was.

"Leave me alone, Holden," she said just as the whistle sounded again and a crew of no less than eight men rounded the corner up ahead. They wore helmets and backpacks, repelling gear and strong hiking boots.

Eden reached them first, and a couple of them immediately set to work checking her out. Holden stayed where he was, this time giving Eden the distance she clearly wanted.

"Sir," one of the men said, making Holden flinch. He looked at the other man, the removal of his gaze from Eden almost painful.

"I'm fine," he said.

"We need to check you out," the other man said.

"I'm Aaron Burr, and I'm a paramedic. I understand you've had some trouble with your leg."

Holden had some trouble with his leg, yes. And his head.

But by far the most painful injury he'd amassed was in his heart, which beat out a message that he may have just lost Eden forever.

CHAPTER ELEVEN

*E*den let the rescue team surround her. Put blankets around her shoulders even though it was plenty warm outside. Feed her. Shove water bottles at her. It had never felt so good to drink from a bottle before, and Eden did it eagerly.

Anything to get the sting of betrayal out of her heart. Her muscles. Her very bones radiated with the ache of Holden's silence.

He might not have lied, but he certainly hadn't said anything either. And to think, she'd gone on and on about the billionaire investors she'd met with, how she wanted to get her outdoor survival gear line started, all of it.

Foolishness had tears pricking her eyes, and one of the men put his arm around her and led her away from the group. "You're okay," he said in a calm, soothing voice. "Tell me where it hurts."

She lifted her wrist and let him rotate it carefully. He looked at her ankle, again putting it through the full range of motion. "We'll take you to the hospital when we get down," he said. "Just to be sure. But I don't think anything's broken or fractured."

Eden couldn't point to her heart and have the paramedic check that out. What tool would he even use?

Why had she allowed herself to hope she and Holden could have a second chance?

Before she could spiral too deeply into her self-loathing, she straightened her shoulders and said, "I think I just want to get down. Can we go, or do we have to wait for everyone?"

"Let me get a crew, and we'll go with you." The man turned back to the three others who'd stayed back to help her. She couldn't help looking up the path to find Holden had sat down, and he had four people working around him too.

With all those bodies between them, she couldn't meet his eye. She didn't want to anyway.

They'd only been up in the mountains together for two days. She could erase them from her memory and go right back to her old life. She hadn't fallen in love with him all over again, not after only two days.

She was fine.

The paramedic returned with his crew, and two of them went in front of her, with two behind. She wasn't the one who needed help, but she allowed them to buffer her from the rest of the world.

The environment. Holden.

And when she got to the bottom of the mountain—the press.

They surged forward, their cameras clicking and their questions being hurled toward her. When they realized she was alone—and not Holden—their interest waned. She knew she wasn't anyone important, but it still stung to have it be so blatantly obvious that her survival was second to Holden's.

She also knew *she* was the reason he was still alive. Whether anyone knew it or not, he'd have been dead in that cave without her.

After answering a few questions for the State Park Ranger, she was allowed to go to her car and leave. She did so, passing the rendezvous point for the path where Holden had parked just as he and his crew arrived at the mouth of the path.

She almost felt bad for him, having to face all those cameras and answer all those questions by himself.

"Almost," she whispered. That seemed to be the theme of her life, and she made a quick decision to go to her parents' house to shower and relax instead of her own. Iris had said everyone had gathered there, and Eden needed the love and support only her family could provide.

"I JUST CAN'T BELIEVE IT," HER MOTHER SAID for at least the twentieth time. She shook her head, the disbelief that had settled into the lines around her eyes still there. "Who wants another cookie?"

No one answered, and she went into the kitchen anyway, leaving Eden alone with her sisters. Their father had gone into the backyard after the first hour of Eden's tale. To be fair, she had started answering questions she'd already answered at that point, and she was tired of talking.

She leaned back into the couch and closed her eyes, a sigh leaking from her mouth.

"You and Holden Holstein," Iris said, plenty of undertones in her voice. "What happened with that?"

Eden could still feel his lips against hers when she said, "Nothing. He's as stubborn as ever, that's what happened with that."

And secretive.

She couldn't believe he owned the company she worked for. But it seemed like the whole world hadn't known that. Dean Black was listed on the website as the company's chief executive officer, but when Holden had gone out to "clear his head" one day and not come back, Dean had done exactly what Holden had said he would.

He'd gone to the cops and the media. She and Holden had been the biggest news story in Getaway Bay since that prince had come to the island, gotten married, and stayed. As if she ranked up there with royalty.

Not only that, but the journalists on the island had a way of digging up dirt if there was any to be found, and it had only taken one night for them to figure out that Dean wasn't the owner of Explore Getaway Bay, but Holden Holstein, who'd also just received a "large inheritance" from his father, the famous cattle rancher on the island.

In short, he was a billionaire, and he would've been on her list to approach about investing in her products. After all, she invented outdoor survival products, and he owned an outdoor tourism company.

It was ironic, really.

In any other situation, she'd have laughed about it. Said, "Can you believe it?" to her sisters and friends. But when it was her on the other end of the deal, she just felt like she'd been stabbed over and over again.

"I think something happened," Orchid said, and Eden's eyes flew open.

"It really didn't," Eden said, leaning forward. She cut a glance toward the kitchen, but her mother was still scooping dough balls onto the cookie sheet. "Fine, something happened." Her sisters leaned in, ultimate curiosity on their faces, even Ivy, who usually stayed out of as much drama as possible.

"I saved his life," Eden whispered. "You should've *seen* his leg. So red and swollen and infected. And I punctured it and drained all the pus—"

"Ew," Iris said, scowling. "Enough."

Eden grinned around at them, determined to keep her two-day affair with her ex-boyfriend a secret until the day she died. After all, it wouldn't do any good to sit around and wish things were different. She'd tried that once, five years ago, and it hadn't gotten her anywhere.

"Were you scared?" Ivy asked, and Eden's eyes flew to her youngest sister's.

"Yeah," she said. "Of course. But we found food and water, and once it stopped raining, it was just a matter of waiting for them to fix the broken path." Eden spoke so matter-of-factly, but the truth was, she hadn't been as scared with Holden as she would've been had she been alone.

She might have tried riskier things to get down. She probably wouldn't have gone up to the spring at all, and she couldn't even imagine how hungry she'd have been. As it was, she felt an ache in her ankle she should have gone to the hospital to get checked. Her head ached. And a wave of exhaustion rolled through her.

She stood and went into the kitchen, giving her mom a side hug with the words, "I'm tired. I'm going to take some pills and go to bed. Can I sleep here for a while?"

"Of course, sweetie." Her mom looked up at her with the same bright blue eyes Eden had. "I'm so glad you're okay." She glanced into the living room. "You should've seen Orchid. She nearly fell apart again."

Sadness swept through Eden. "I'm sorry. I didn't mean to get stuck up there."

"She knows that. We all know that. It just hit home for her."

Eden gathered the medicine she needed and a fresh water bottle from the fridge before giving each of her sisters a hug and heading down the hall to the guest bedroom where she and Orchid used to sleep as little girls.

Once behind the safety of the closed door, Eden swallowed all the pills and looked around. Orchid had stayed here for a few months after the death of her husband, and it definitely had the vibe of a grown woman and a little girl.

Her husband had died in a fishing boat accident, leaving Orchid and an unborn baby behind. That baby was now six-year-old Tesla, and Orchid worked as an office administrator for a flower company on the island. Ironically.

Eden moved over to the bed and sat on the end of it, everything storming through her. She probably shouldn't be alone right now, but she didn't want to answer any more questions or make up any more stories about how nothing had happened with Holden.

Because *some*thing had happened.

She'd opened her heart to him again. He'd unlocked the door so easily too, reached right in and taken her most vital organ.

Tears splashed her cheeks, but she made no move to

wipe them away or quell them. Just like Mother Nature had blown herself out a couple of days ago, Eden had a storm inside her that needed to be released.

Later, after she'd slept and eaten dinner with her parents, she went back to her own house. When she turned the corner, a sea of cars and vans spread before her. As she inched between them, she realized what was going on.

The media had found her. Why they cared now when they hadn't that morning, she wasn't sure. What she knew was when she pulled into her driveway and got out of her car, over a dozen people had magically appeared on the sidewalk in front of her house.

"Is it true you saved Holden Holstein's life?" one asked.

"How many outdoor survival products have you made?" another shouted.

"Can we see the can cooker that you collected rain-water in?" asked a third.

Eden just stood there, unsure of what to say. She wasn't the one with experience in front of cameras and microphones. With a start, she realized Holden wasn't either. That was why he let Dean be the public face of Explore Getaway Bay.

"Excuse me," she said, her voice barely more than a peep. She turned and went up her front steps, effectively shutting out the shouted questions and desperate pleas for an interview.

They knew about the inventions. Had Holden told them about her shed too?

Anger flowed through her. He had no right to tell anyone anything about her. She didn't need her failure splashed all over the front page of The Island News, thank you very much.

She plugged in her phone and turned it on, a shiver running through her. She adjusted the air conditioning so it wasn't quite so cold and spun when her phone chimed. Maybe it was Holden, apologizing for everything and asking her when they could get that dinner.

She hesitated. She wouldn't go to that dinner. She'd make some excuse for why she couldn't be there only a few minutes before they were supposed to meet. Or something.

She did check her phone, her disappointment only that much more painful when the text wasn't from Holden at all. So he'd told the press all about her, probably to get them off his back, and then he'd gone right back into hiding.

And if there was one thing Eden knew Holden was very good at, it was hiding.

CHAPTER TWELVE

*B*y the time Holden finally stepped out of the shower, most of the hot water was gone, and he'd kept Dean waiting for an hour. He didn't care. Because of what his best friend had done, Holden had been delayed in getting home, getting behind closed doors, getting clean by hours and hours.

He didn't even know that many reporters lived and worked on the island. So many cameras. He shuddered at the thought of the pictures that would surely be on the Internet already. The news that night. And in the paper in the morning.

Eden had gone ahead of him, and by the time he'd gotten down to the trailhead, she'd been completely gone. Frustration filled him as he padded down the hall and into his kitchen, where Dean had made coffee and ordered pizza.

Holden was grateful for both, and as Willie came

trotting over to him, Holden carefully crouched down and hugged his dog. "Hey, bud," he whispered into the dog's scruff. "You doin' okay? Yeah, I'm okay too."

Dean came in from the deck, his eyes filled with concern. "You didn't go to the hospital."

"No," Holden said, turning away from his best friend, business partner, and only lifeline back to normal life after the death of his mother.

"Why not?"

"The paramedics on the mountain said I should, but I could probably wait if I didn't want to go today." He poured himself a cup of coffee and slid his eyes past Dean to get the cream out of the fridge. "And I didn't want to go today."

His leg didn't hurt that bad. They'd given him a steroid shot with antibiotics before they'd let him hike down on his own. And he sure wasn't going to let them carry him out. The pictures the media had gotten would be bad enough.

The silence in his too-big house felt stifling, suffocating. He loaded a plate with food, and he walked toward Dean, making sure he didn't limp nearly at all. They both went out onto the deck, and Holden could finally breathe again.

"You okay?" Dean asked, and Holden appreciated the concern in his friend's voice.

"I was out there with Eden," Holden said very quietly. He filled his mouth with food, somewhat surprised Eden hadn't called or texted yet. If he had money to bet—and he did—she'd gone to her parents' house instead of going home first.

She might even spend the night there. He hoped she would, and he vowed not to contact her until morning. Give her time to cool off a little. The sarcasm and bitterness in her last words to him still reverberated around inside his ears, no matter how hard he tried to forget them.

"And?" Dean prompted when Holden didn't expound.

"And I want to try again with her." He sighed and finished his piece of pizza. "But I screwed up. I didn't tell her about Explore Getaway Bay, and she has this whole line of survival products...." He trailed off, because he didn't need to repeat the story. Dean had been at the scene when Holden had come off the trail. He'd heard his statement to the press about Eden being the genius with the supplies, how Eden had saved his life, how her outdoor survival products should be in everyone's backpacks.

"You probably didn't need to call in the Navy SEALs," he added.

"Justin's a friend," Dean said with a wave of his hand. Like, *no big deal.*

But to Holden, it was a big deal. The SEALs had drawn a lot of attention, and yes, they'd rebuilt the path in such a way that it would probably never fall again. But it just wasn't necessary. Not for him.

"And he's technically not a SEAL anymore," Dean said. "He retired a few months ago."

"He's a SEAL," Holden said.

Dean let a few seconds go by in silence. He watched Holden eat another piece of pizza, and then another. "Are you telling me you're hung up on Eden?"

"No," Holden said. "Yes. Maybe?" He had no idea. "It was nice to be reminded that she...cared about me once."

"So what happened?"

Never one to kiss and tell, Holden danced around the edges of what had really happened on Bald Mountain Cliffs. "She took care of me," he said. "She saved my leg, and probably my life. She found food, and she got us water, and she had a phone."

"She should be our spokesperson for Explore GB," Dean said, not a hint of teasing in sight.

A light bulb lit up in Holden's head. "You're right. She should." He frowned. "Do you think she'd do that?"

"I have no idea. How bad did you leave things?"

What a joke. Those had been her last words to him. "Not well," he said, thinking he was probably estimating high at that.

"And even though Eden has blonde hair, she has the temper of a redhead," Dead said with a smile. "So maybe let me talk to her."

"I want to talk to her," Holden said. "And I want to

propose to the board that we buy her line of outdoor survival products."

Dean's eyebrows went up. "Have you seen them?"

"In action," he said. "And no Swiss Army knife would've cut that walking stick for me." Honestly, it didn't matter if her inventions weren't that great. The fact was, she'd survived out in the wilderness with them, and that alone would make them fly off the shelves.

"Put together the proposal," he said. "We'll take it to the next board meeting."

"That's not until next month." He hadn't been briefed on the one he'd missed yesterday morning, but if he knew Dean—and he did—they'd be having that talk next.

"Gives you time to get everything in line." Dean smiled at him. "About yesterday, we need to talk about the possibility of voting Jean out at the next election meeting."

Holden snorted. "That will never happen. She owns fifteen percent of the company."

"I think we can get her daughter to take her place." Dean lifted his eyebrows and reached for his bottle of soda.

"You do? And you think Jessica is a better option that her mother?" Because Holden did not think that.

"She at least listens," Dean said. "Joan has an agenda, and she doesn't hear a word anyone else says."

"True." Holden didn't want to talk business. He

didn't want to think about Eden. He just wanted to sleep. So he said, "Thanks for everything, Dean," and went down the hall to his bedroom.

When he woke in the morning, he almost didn't know where he was. The ground around him was so soft, and he didn't know why. Had they found somewhere less rocky to sleep?

He turned over, expecting to find Eden there.

His eyes flew open, and he realized he wasn't out in the wilderness with her anymore. And it was the next morning, which meant he'd kept his promise to himself.

He texted her, something simple. *Hey there. Hope you got home okay.* He just needed to get the door open again. Get her talking to him again.

She didn't respond. An hour passed, and his phone remained silent. By lunchtime, he was logging into the Explore Getaway Bay employee database to find out where she'd been assigned to work.

Maybe she'd have called in today. If he had an app, he'd know that.

Or maybe, she'd be on the submarine tour where she'd been assigned. They left every hour, on the hour, and that meant he had forty-nine minutes to get over to the docking station.

EDEN WAS NOT AT THE SUBMARINE DOCK. Little children and families ran rampant everywhere, but the girl he talked to at the ticket window said Eden had called in sick that day. Holden was a tiny bit surprised. Eden acted like nothing fazed her, but something on that mountain had.

He hoped it was him at the same time he prayed it wasn't.

He wasn't sixteen years old, and he couldn't just slowly drive by her house to see if her car was in the driveway. What would he do then? Go knock on her door?

No, Holden wasn't that kind of man, and he ended up going back to his place behind the gates in a community at the base of the bluffs.

She still hadn't answered him, and Holden spent the rest of the day starting a proposal for the board about Eden's outdoor survival products. No, he hadn't seen them all. He was sure what Eden had brought with her on a simple day hike hadn't even scratched the surface of what she'd invented in that shed in her backyard.

He wanted to call her. Hear her voice. See if he could get inside the shed.

But he wouldn't use his money and position and the possibility of her getting the funding she'd been trying to secure to get her to talk to him. That wouldn't be fair, and Holden didn't want that between them.

Besides, the shareholders could say no. Joan would definitely vote no.

Now, she might suggest they bring in Eden as a consultant, and the fact that she already worked for the company was a huge benefit.

His phone rang, and he practically lunged for it. But it wasn't Eden.

"Dad," he said after answering the call. "What's going on?" His father usually only called when something happened.

"I saw you made it down safely," he said, as if Holden has just gotten off the trail an hour ago.

"Yeah," he said. "Yesterday."

"I thought I might see you today."

Holden pressed his lips together. "Sorry, Dad," he said. "I've just been resting."

"You know, Lincoln went through something similar."

"I'd actually forgotten about that." His half-brother had been lost at sea, crashed on a deserted island. Holden wondered what products Eden had for something like that. He didn't even know what that would be like. Surrounded by water, none of it drinkable.

He silently vowed never to get on a ship or boat again without desalination tablets in his pockets. Heck, he should probably start to carry a backpack of supplies around with him everywhere he went.

"We're wondering if you want to grab dinner

tonight." His dad sounded casual, but Holden heard something in the undertone of his voice.

Holden's first reaction was to say no. He was busy. He had a proposal to work on. Any number of excuses came to mind. But instead of using them, he said, "Sure. What time were you thinking?"

After all, the board didn't meet again for weeks. He had plenty of time to get the proposal polished and prepared. So perfect, even Joan wouldn't be able to find fault with it.

CHAPTER THIRTEEN

*E*den took a few days off work, deciding she could afford to sleep in and make sure her body and mind were rested.

Holden had texted each morning for five straight days, but Eden didn't know how to answer him. Each message was simple and short.

Hope you got home okay.

Does it feel as weird to you to wake up in bed instead of on the ground?

Finally went to the doctor for my leg. He says I'm all good. Thank you.

Eden was glad Holden wouldn't have any lasting trouble with his leg. She wasn't surprised he'd waited to go to the doctor. The man was as stubborn as the day was long. And yet, he'd done what she'd asked him to as well. He'd taken the pills. Eaten her food. All of it.

She tinkered in her shed in the mornings before it

got too terribly hot. Soon enough, it wouldn't matter what time of day she went out. The day started hot in the summer. Eden usually thrived on that, the glorious, bright sun one of the reasons she loved Hawaii so much.

The hype from her and Holden's experience died down. The press disappeared off her front lawn, apparently satisfied with the story they'd managed to get. She went back to work, and life marched on.

Her house was a little quieter than she remembered. Her life a little more empty, even when she worked on the submarine.

At least she hadn't said anything bad about her job. About Holden's company. *Getaway Bay's newest billionaire.*

Every time she thought of that, foolishness raced through her, hot and fast. By the second week, she'd managed to just feel disappointed she hadn't known about him and his status. She might have had the best shot to get funding for her products through Explore Getaway Bay and Holden.

But she certainly wasn't going to ask now.

Holden had stopped texting too, and while part of her wanted him to let her slip quietly away, the other part of her wanted him to show up on her doorstep and fight for her. Fight for them.

"You've got a letter," Cotton said one day when Eden stopped by the office to check her schedule. He waved the envelope at her, but Eden frowned. She didn't get mail at the office. She came in once a week to make sure her hours got logged right and check what she'd been assigned to do the following week.

"From who?" she asked.

"Explore GB."

Eden crossed over to the bank of interoffice mailboxes. She honestly never got anything here. Maybe her tax documents in January. The slip of paper that was supposed to serve as the official invitation to the company beach bash. Stuff like that.

But this envelope looked official, like what her paychecks used to come in before the company went digital. Her thoughts turned to Holden and the app he'd claimed the company would be getting. Maybe that had stolen his attention from her. After all, the man really worked two jobs.

"Open it," Cotton said when she just stood there, staring at it.

"Did you get one?" she asked.

"Nope."

She scanned the rows and columns of boxes. "Did anyone else get one?"

"Nope." Cotton grinned at her. "It was hand-delivered, just a few minutes ago."

"By who?"

Cotton shrugged, though by the edge in his eye, he knew. "Just open it."

Eden wanted to do it in private, but Cotton certainly wasn't going anywhere. So she ripped the flap up and pulled out a thick piece of paper with official Explore Getaway Bay letterhead on it.

She read quickly, her stomach sinking with every sentence. "The board wants me at their next meeting." She handed the paper—which probably cost as much as her groceries for the week—to Cotton.

He read it too, his smile fading by the end. "Why do you think the board wants you to come to their meeting?"

"It says to give an official report about what happened on Bald Mountain Cliffs."

"Can't they just get the police report?"

"Good question." Eden turned away from him and the mailboxes and stepped over to the computer where employees checked their schedules. It would be emailed out on Sunday night, but Eden liked to know which days she had off and which tours she was doing. She'd been packing a backpack with her everywhere she went, as she sometimes drove the safaris Jeeps out into the wilderness areas of the island. And if she and some tourists got stuck out there….

She tapped and scrolled down to the Ms to find her name. "I'm not scheduled to work?" Straightening, she looked around as if the shift manager would be there to answer her question.

Ryan wasn't there. He arrived at nine on the dot and left at five. Eden had been at Lightning Point that day, taking people through the lighthouse there and explaining how petrified lightning was made. The popular place to visit sat around the island, a good half an hour from the main part of town, and she was definitely later than five o'clock.

"Maybe Anna has you on private tours," Cotton said.

"Why doesn't it say that then?" Eden stepped back and let Cotton look at the schedule.

"And it says paid," he said. "Which is like you put in for vacation days."

"I didn't," she said. "I don't need next week off." In fact, Eden took very little time off. "I'll call him." She dialed Ryan, hoping he was having a good evening. Sometimes he could be snappy, especially if his twins were acting up. Eden had no idea how to deal with two six-year-old boys at the same time, so she usually gave Ryan a lot of slack.

"Hey, Eden," he said, and he sounded like he could have a conversation.

Eden asked, "Do you have a quick minute?"

"Sure," he said.

"I'm not on the schedule for next week."

"Oh, right." He cleared his throat. "I probably should've texted you."

"Okay," she said, waiting for more of an explanation than that.

"The board meets next week."

"On Thursday," she said, glancing at the discarded letter on the counter. "I heard."

"They requested I give you the week off."

"Why?"

"I don't know."

She picked up the letter again, thinking maybe it had the agenda for the board meeting. A clue as to why she needed the whole week off for a meeting on Thursday morning.

"You're not losing any pay," Ryan said. "And they said they'd comp the vacation days, so they don't count against you either."

Before Eden knew Holden ran this company, she'd have been confused out of her mind. But as Ryan spoke, everything came together. "Thank you, Ryan," she said. "Sorry to bother you at home."

"My fault," he said. "I should've texted you."

Eden hung up and immediately dialed Holden. When he answered with an immediate, "Hey there," she almost lost her nerve.

Thankfully, her mouth knew what to do.

"You gave me the whole week off for a Thursday morning board meeting?"

"Yes," he said simply.

"I don't need a week off," she said, rolling her eyes at Cotton. "What am I going to do all week?" She'd be bored out of her mind. Didn't Holden know boredom was her number one fear?

"Prepare for the meeting," he said, his voice even and seemingly un-frustrated.

"Why?" she asked. "What am I doing there?"

"I'd like you to bring a few of your outdoor survival

products to show them."

The words landed like bombs in Eden's ears. "I have to present?"

"You're great at public speaking," he said. "Just think of it as a tour out at Lightning Point."

So he knew where she was. He'd probably checked her schedule every week, same as she had. Eden wasn't sure why her heart was beating so fast. Probably a warning not to get involved with Holden again. It was likely telling her to run.

"Holden," she said, the tiniest bit of a whine in her voice.

"Please don't say my name like that," he said, and he did sound strained around the edges now. "The meeting is at nine o'clock. I'm assuming you know where the corporate office building is."

"Yes," she said, because she didn't know what else to say. Could he have real feelings for her?

So what if he does? she asked herself. He'd stopped texting in the morning, and perhaps they simply weren't meant to be.

"I'd arrive a little early," he said.

"Okay," she said, not sure how to end this call.

"See you then," he said, and the call ended.

She let her arm drop to her side, more confused than ever.

"What's going on?" Cotton asked, stepping in front of her.

"He wants me to present my outdoor survival products to the board. Says I need time to prepare, so he gave me the week off."

Cotton frowned at her. "Seems weird."

"Right?" Eden wasn't going to argue with Holden though. It wouldn't do much good, and she couldn't help feeling hopeful about her and Holden. Hopeful that she might have finally found the right investor for her products.

Her phone chimed, and she glanced at a message from Anna. *You're off all of next week? You can't take any groups?*

In the weeks since her stranded experience, Eden had been right about her friends. Cotton and Anna had reached out to her over and over, and a rush of gratitude filled her. She looked up at Cotton, who still wore concern in his expression.

"I gotta go." She hugged him, a surprising move for Eden, who maybe wasn't as touchy-feely as other people.

On the way out of the building, she texted Anna back. *What day is the group? I have a few things to get ready for, but I'm sure I can squeeze them in.*

THURSDAY CAME AS IF MONDAY, TUESDAY, AND Wednesday had been removed from the calendar. She'd gotten no further instructions from Holden, but she knew enough about board meetings to show up in a cute skirt and blouse, along with a folder in one hand and a small box in the other. People didn't go to meetings without folders and boxes, right?

She asked how to get to the board meeting, and the man at the desk in the lobby put her on a private elevator that went straight to the top floor. Once there, a woman in a red dress and heels greeted her, offered her water, and had her sit on the couch.

Everywhere Eden looked, she saw glass. All the rooms off the hallway had windows looking into them, and she didn't think she could ever work in an environment like this. She did enjoy the air conditioning, and everyone who walked by wore dress clothes and smiles.

So maybe she could work here.

You're not going to work here, she told herself. What would she do? Run out and get coffee for the more important people? No, thanks.

Nine o'clock came and went, and no one came to get her. She finally stood up and approached the desk where the woman in the red dress worked. "Should I...?"

"They know you're here," she said, her plastic smile in place. "Mister Holstein said he'd come get you when they were ready for you."

"Oh, okay." Eden wandered back to the couch, taking her time as she glanced down the hallway. She was hoping to catch a glimpse of anyone in any sort of meeting, but she couldn't. And now with the woman in the red dress watching her, she didn't dare go exploring.

Another fifteen minutes passed, and she wondered why Holden had told her to be early. Finally, movement appeared in her peripheral vision, and she turned that way.

She stood, her breath catching somewhere behind her lungs. Holden stood there, buttoning his suit coat, and he looked mighty fine. The jacket had to be tailor-made just for him, as his shoulders seemed impossibly wide.

"Eden," he said, his voice reaching right down into her stomach and pulling. "We're ready for you." He gestured down a completely different hallway than where she'd been looking. She held her head high and drew in a deep breath. After smoothing her skirt and collecting her box, she walked toward him, her fingers tight on that useless folder.

In any other building, she'd have been able to duck around the corner and get some privacy. She couldn't believe she was thinking of kissing him.

The clean, fresh scent of him met her nose as she slipped past him and into the next hall, further muddling her thoughts. "Straight ahead," he said.

She walked, feeling very much like she might not survive her experience in the courtroom. Pausing, she turned back to Holden. Their eyes met, and so many things were said in that moment.

Some things had to be said out loud, though.

"Thank you," she said in a voice hardly loud enough for her own ears to hear.

Then she turned again and marched forward, wishing she'd worn heels instead of the sensible sandals on her feet.

CHAPTER FOURTEEN

*H*olden's mouth felt like he'd swallowed a strange mixture of sand paper and cotton balls. He needed a drink—again—and every swallow scratched.

Thank you.

Eden looked brilliant and powerful as she entered the room and went straight to the head of the table, the screen behind her already illuminated from the presentation he'd just finished.

If the board didn't approve his acquisition of Eden's products, he'd buy them himself. His belief in her had only strengthened in the last month, even though she'd never responded to any of his texts.

"Ladies and gentlemen," he said, his smooth business meeting voice back in place. Thankfully. "This is Eden McLaughlin. I've asked her to come show you a few things." He nodded at her to begin and took a seat beside her.

She tucked her hair behind her ear, and he remembered doing such a thing too. His heart hurt to see her, breathe her in, and not be able to touch her. She took her time opening the box, and then she proceeded to speak in a clear, concise way that had pride flowing through him.

Her products got passed around, and a few people took notes. Eden only spoke for about ten minutes, and then she looked at him again.

"Any questions?" he asked, realizing he'd just opened the door to the lion's den, and it was feeding time. He probably should've warned Eden what the board could be like.

"You already work for Explore Getaway Bay," Thomas said. "Is that right?"

"Yes, sir." Eden didn't look at Holden for his approval, and that only made him admire her more. He had to get her back into his life, and his stomach pinched at what was still to come.

"Can this be easily manufactured?" Lilianna asked, lifting up the can cooker.

"I don't see why not," Eden said. "It's a can with a shelf under it. I made it in my shed with a little bit of welding magic."

"How much does welding magic cost?" someone asked, and several people chuckled—including Eden.

"I didn't put together pricing," she said. "I'm afraid

I don't really know how much it would take to reproduce products like these." She swallowed, the first sign of her nerves, and looked at Holden.

"I've already presented you with a list of costs," he said, standing up and buttoning his jacket again. "From what I knew, of course. We can work more closely with Miss McLaughlin to get things more on track if the proposal is approved."

He saw all the questions run through Eden's eyes, the biggest being *Proposal? What proposal?*

"Should we vote?" Dean asked, and Holden shot him a look of appreciation. "We don't want to take up all of Miss McLaughlin's time."

The vote was called for, and Holden tapped on his computer to bring up the proposal again, twisting to make sure the words shone on the screen. He moved out of the way, touching Eden's elbow lightly to get her to come with him.

She did, and when they were standing on the side, she looked up at the screen. He heard her suck in a breath and hold it. Heard him whisper, "Holden." But he needed this vote to happen first, so he didn't turn toward her. Didn't respond to his name. He simply nodded at Dean.

"On the proposal that we fund, manufacture, and sell Eden McLaughlin's line of outdoor survival products, exclusively through Explore Getaway Bay online and retail establishments where they currently exist, and where they might exist in the future, who votes yes?"

Holden didn't dare look around the table. He reached for Eden's hand and held it, squeezing tight.

The best part? She squeezed back.

"And no?" Dean glanced around the table, a smile forming on his face. "The vote is fourteen to one in favor, sir."

Holden beamed around at the board seated at the table. "Thank you, ladies and gentlemen."

"With the stipulation in place," Thomas reminded him, and Holden nodded.

"Of course."

"That's it for today," Dean said next, and Holden tugged on Eden's hand to get her to come with him. People started filing out the door and into the hallway, chatter breaking out. He knew several of them would want to talk to Eden, congratulate her, but he had to talk to her first.

Now.

He led her through a door in the back of the room and into the office there. Not his, but he and Dean used the room for a board meeting homebase, and the surface of the desk was covered in paper and empty soda cans.

He didn't care what Eden thought of the mess. As soon as the door closed behind her and they were alone, Holden swept her into his arms. "You got it," he whispered, the soft, floral scent of her hair almost overwhelming him. "We even cracked Joan." He chuckled, feeling like spinning around and laughing.

His enthusiasm and joy dissolved when he realized Eden was crying against his chest. "Hey," he said, stroking her hair. "What's wrong?"

She pulled away, sniffling and wiping her face. "You bought my products."

"Yes," he said, confused at the accusation in her eyes. "I thought that's what you wanted. We'll manufacture them and put them in every gift shop and retail space on the island that we have. Your cut is huge, Eden, I promise. The biggest I've ever seen a business grant. And they did it without even questioning it."

He peered down into her face. "Wasn't this what you wanted?"

She nodded, still wiping her eyes. "Yes. Thank you, Holden."

Feeling as if he might not survive the next five minutes of conversation, Holden took a breath. "I'll admit, this was only a ploy to get you to talk to me."

Their eyes met, and that same lightning-hot attraction that had always existed between them burst to life.

"I want the products, sure. But what I really want, is you." He reached for her hand, somewhat surprised she let him take it. "I desperately miss you. I'm in love with you. I'll do whatever it takes to get you back."

She softened considerably, but he wasn't finished yet. "I'm sorry, Eden. I should've told you what I really did for a living while we were out on that mountain.

There were opportunities. I just...." He blew out his breath. He didn't want to make excuses. Not to her.

"I just didn't." He took a micro-step toward her. "Can you forgive me?"

"Do you even work for The Web Developer?"

"Tuesday through Friday," he said. "Dean and I meet on Mondays, and of course, I have to attend this horrible board meeting every first Thursday of the month." He smiled, hoping he could elicit one from her too.

Slowly—oh, so slowly—that smile bloomed to life on her face.

"So you hired yourself to do the app."

Eden never missed much, and Holden shrugged. "I suppose."

"What's the stipulation?" she asked.

Of course she hadn't missed that. "The board wants you to come to the corporate office and act as a consultant and training coach on wilderness survival for the company."

"A what and a what?"

Holden laughed, drawing her back into his arms. "I have everything for you in a folder here somewhere."

"I knew people brought folders to meetings," she said.

She fit so perfectly in his arms, and Holden had to know how she felt about him. "So? What do you think?"

"I think I'm going to need to buy fancier dresses

and my first pair of high heels."

Holden looked down into those ocean-colored eyes, ready to dive all the way in. "I meant about us." He pressed his lips to her forehead, enjoying the way she leaned into his touch. That told him something, but not enough.

"About my apology. My plea for you to forgive me." He touched his lips to the corner of her eye. Then her cheek, steadily working his way toward her mouth. "I want to go to dinner with you, like we talked about on the cliffs. I want to lay by you on the beach. I want you to meet my dog. Come see my new house. Oh, that's another one for the game we were playing. I got a new house."

Eden's eyes were closed, and she felt and looked like an angel to him. "Eden?" he whispered.

"Kiss me already," she whispered back, and Holden didn't waste another moment before brushing his mouth against hers.

"I'm sorry," he murmured against her lips, claiming them in a deeper kiss the second time.

"I'm sorry too," she said, this in-between game of talking one of his favorites of theirs so far.

"You forgive me?" He kissed her, the feel of her fingernails in his hair absolutely magical.

"Yes," she said, pressing fully into him now.

"I love you," he whispered, their lips barely parting.

She kissed him and kissed him and kissed him before she finally said, "I love you, too, Holden."

CHAPTER FIFTEEN

*E*den sat under the umbrella while Holden put their tacos on the table and slid next to her. She buried her sandaled feet in the sand, this day turning out so different than she'd planned.

Holden had prepared an entire proposal without telling her. He'd negotiated a position for her higher up in the company, where she could work with a team to develop her products, as well as lead educational training on wilderness survival for the tour guides at Explore Getaway Bay, and the public.

It was her dream job. Tinker with her inventions whenever she wanted. Talk to people about being prepared when they went out hiking. A win-win.

And the gorgeous man beside her, his suit coat discarded somewhere so he was only in his short sleeves and a loose tie? Absolutely sexy, and the best part of her life.

"You're not hungry?" he asked, nudging the box of tacos closer to her. "I got eight of these. Eat one."

"I don't want to eat your food," she said, and his eyes flew to hers. She giggled, and he shook his head as he smiled.

"You'll eat it if I have to stuff it in your mouth and move your jaw for you." He cocked his eyebrow at her. "Not so fun when it's you, is it?"

She burst out laughing, her blonde hair falling over her shoulders as her head tipped back. Maybe she forgave too easily. But if that was what anyone accused her of, she decided she could live with it.

After all, the man had just bought her ideas and offered her a better job.

And better yet, he'd offered her himself. Eden could admit he was all she wanted, and she didn't care about the number of zeroes in his bank account or where this new house was.

He leaned over and kissed her, stealing the laughter from her throat at the same time he silenced her.

"Mm," she said. "Those tacos do taste good."

He slid the box a little closer to her, and she picked one up. "Does this count as the dinner?"

"No," he said. "This is lunch."

"Are you going to take me to dinner tonight?"

"Absolutely."

"Can I see where you develop apps?"

"Sure."

"And your house."

"Before or after dinner?" He looked at her out of the corner of his eyes, and all Eden could think about was going back to his place after dinner and kissing him until her lips bruised.

"Either," she said, trying to erase the fantasies from her mind.

"Let's see how the afternoon plays out," he said, further loosening his tie. "I have to get out of these clothes, so we'll probably go back to the house before dinner."

"Out of those clothes?"

He pulled at his tie again, unbuttoning his top button. "I'm choking."

She laughed and ate her taco, so glad this Thursday had turned out better than she'd been imagining.

She did get to see the app and give him her opinion on it. She got the grand tour of his house and met his dog. She kissed him in the kitchen, the hallway, and her own front porch when he finally dropped her off at home.

The next few weeks became a blur of new things. New experiences of shopping for professional clothes, including the cute shoes she'd thought she'd hate. She didn't hate them, and now she clicked around the glass corporate building with real folders of information in her hand.

New trainings for her new job. New materials and upgraded designs for her products. New, new, new.

But she kept her old friends, and more important, her old boyfriend.

Eden established a routine, one of her favorite things, and she woke each morning with a smile on her face, ready for whatever excitement her new life would bring her. She realized that yes, she'd loved her old job. Loved doing the tours and talking to families and tourists.

But she really, really loved doing her wilderness safety classes, both with the public and with Explore Getaway Bay employees. She really loved going down to the engineering department and seeing how they were coming on the product line, which should be ready to launch just after the New Year.

She'd had no idea it would take more than six months to get a few outdoor survival products ready, but she should've known Holden wouldn't do anything halfway.

He asked as many questions as she did about materials and price points, and he insisted they use the best steel, the best cord, the best of everything in the product. "This is Explore Getaway Bay," he'd said, his eyes hooking hers and refusing to let go. "We only want the best."

She'd kissed him after that meeting, and he'd asked her how she felt about marriage.

"I feel great about marriage," she said, still holding onto his shoulders. "Do you...I mean. I didn't think you wanted to get married."

"Depends," he said.

"On what?" she asked.

"On who I'm asking." He'd kissed her again, on the first floor in the engineering department, and Eden felt sure he'd ask her to marry him soon.

But another month passed. He spent Thanksgiving with her family, which she enjoyed.

And another month passed. No proposal. No ring. Not even another mention of the word marriage.

She cleared space in the retail store on the first floor of the Explore Getaway Bay corporate headquarters, because her products were launching soon.

Next week, in fact.

She stood back and looked at the shelf space where their new products would go. *Her* new products.

A sense of accomplishment filled her, and she covered her mouth with one hand, awe striking her. She'd done it. She'd really found an investor who believed in her and her products.

Well, maybe Holden had found her....

Her phone chimed, and she checked it to find a text from Holden. *Hey there. You're not in your office, and we're meeting for lunch in twenty. Where are you?*

Retail store, she typed out. *I just remembered we were going to lunch with the DuPonts today. Sorry, I forgot. Excited about clearing shelf space for the new products!*

He sent a smiley face emoji and said *Be down in a minute.*

When he emerged from the elevator, he wore more

than his usual jeans and polo. Today, he'd put on khakis and a button-down shirt the color of ripe mangos.

Mangos.

He kissed her, tucked her hand in his, and they set off for the Sweet Breeze Resort and Spa, where they were meeting with Fisher and Stacey DuPont about some billionaire's club Holden had been invited to.

"And you're sure it won't be awkward with there?" Eden asked again. "I asked Fisher for money, and he turned me down."

"His loss," Holden said, getting behind the wheel of his SUV. "And it's fine. They know you're coming, and they're happy about it."

Eden wasn't sure if she was happy about it or not. She wasn't a billionaire, and she didn't think she'd get invited to the meetings. But maybe a billionaire's wife….

She cleared the thought from her mind. She was not Holden's wife. Or even his fiancée.

"I was thinking we should go hiking tomorrow," he said. "A day trip up to the springs?"

She jerked her attention to him. "The springs? Really?"

"I'll pack tons of food and water," he said with that sly, sexy smile. "Painkillers. Antibiotics. The whole nine yards." He pulled into the circle drive at Sweet Breeze. "But I've already checked the weather, and we should be clear." He didn't get out even though the valet stood at his window.

"What do you think?"

"Sure," she said. "I'll bring the can cooker and some lunch."

The next day, Holden arrived way before noon, all suited up for a hike. He had the hat, the backpack, the hiking boots. Eden almost swooned at the very sight of him, but she managed to get her own backpack off the couch and follow him to his truck.

They both paused on the rebuilt part of the trail, and Eden hadn't stopped to admire it on the way down last time. "Wow," she said.

"They were Navy SEALs," he said, toeing the wood and steel beams. "Friends of Dean's."

"Was he a Navy SEAL?"

"His brother was." Holden continued up, and Eden went with him, her hand intertwined with his. The spring didn't seem nearly as far as it had with an injured ankle and the constant worry of Holden's leg in the back of her mind.

They filled their water bottles and drank from the spring before turning to survey the beautiful Hawaiian landscape before them.

"It's beautiful," she murmured.

"You sure are," he said, and she turned toward him at the same time he dropped to one knee. "I'm in love with you, Eden. Because of my dad, I never thought I'd want to marry anyone." He swallowed, his throat working hard. "But I want to marry you. Will you marry me?"

He cracked the ring box he held to reveal a glinting diamond ring nestled among the silk.

Eden sucked in a breath, her heart pounding furiously in her chest. "Holden."

He waited, and Eden basked in the happiness streaming through her. "Yes," she whispered. "Yes, I'll marry you."

Laughter bubbled from his mouth, and he slipped the ring onto her finger. "For a minute there, I thought you were going to say no."

She cradled his face in her hands and kissed him gently. "You thought wrong."

"I love you." He touched his lips to hers again, and Eden let her eyes close all the way as she murmured, "I love you too," and kissed him completely.

Read on for a sneak peek at the next book in the series, **THE OVERBOARD MISTAKE, available now.**

SNEAK PEEK! THE OVERBOARD MISTAKE CHAPTER ONE

*I*ris McLaughlin tapped something on the huge desk calendar in front of her. "And don't forget to get over to Henry's," she said, glancing up at Amelia. "He's twice a week in this heat."

"Twice a week," Amelia deadpanned, because Iris had told her all of this before. Maybe she was a little nervous about leaving the success of her business in someone else's hands.

She'd built We'll Weed That from the ground up, literally. The company had started with her weeding a few people's yards in her time after school back when she was a teenager. She'd incorporated once she'd graduated, and she moved on to complete lawn care. Mowing, weeding, fertilizing, trimming.

A few years later, she'd hired two landscape architects, and her business in Getaway Bay had taken off. She hadn't changed the name, and now We'll Weed

That had a full-scale nursery, as well as unique yard designs to go with their landscaping upkeep.

"Where are Sam and Betty?" she asked, deciding she didn't need to go through the list with Amelia. She looked down the hall as if her general manager and her lead construction guru would appear simply because she wanted them to.

"Probably kissing just outside the back door," Amelia said, her eyes sparkling now.

Iris giggled, though it probably was true. She didn't want to go on this cruise with the happiest couple on earth, but they'd earned the prize. Never mind that she hadn't been out with anyone in eight months and that her sister had just gotten engaged to a billionaire.

Wouldn't that be nice? she thought dryly, though she didn't want to get stuck on Bald Mountain Cliffs for a couple of days the way Eden had. But she would take the handsome boyfriend with loads of money.

Her daydreams continued, and it wasn't until Betty came down the hall with her duffle bag over her shoulder. "Are you coming? We've been outside waiting for you for twenty minutes."

Had it been that long? Iris tended to run late to almost all of her appointments, no matter how early she left. "Coming," she said, tapping the end of her pen on the countertop before ducking into her office to grab her bag.

The three of them drove across Getaway Bay to the dock where the fourteen-day cruise disembarked.

They'd go around all the Hawaiian islands, and out toward a group of islands that could only be seen at certain times of the year. Apparently, the beginning of March was a great time to see whales, dolphins, and the islands, and every email she'd gotten about her cruise had indicated it would be packed full of people.

Iris rode in the back of the company vehicle, her nerves twittering just a little bit. When they arrived at the office, Betty threw her a scathing look and said, "We need to hurry, or they'll give our tickets away."

"They will?"

"You have to check in by ten," Betty said, practically running toward the door. "It's after that already."

Chaos reigned inside the tiny trailer that housed the cruise's office. Iris could barely get inside, and it was clear people wanted to be in here rather than outside because of the misters running and creating a warm, tropical atmosphere.

Betty pressed her way to the counter, and Iris followed her. "Betty Terrace," she said. "Sam Potter. Iris McLaughlin."

The woman there scanned the sheet in front of her, though Iris could clearly see everyone else had checked in. "You barely made it," she said as a bell rang. The crowd started shuffling toward a side door. "That's the bell for the orientation." The woman stamped a piece of paper and started rattling off instructions.

Iris barely listened, because the pull to go with the other bodies called to her. She waited beside Betty, though, until she said, "Great, thanks," grabbed the papers, and hurried after everyone else.

"I'm sorry," Iris said, taking her sheaf of papers from Betty. "I didn't realize what time it was." How much time had she lost romanticizing things in her head? Too much. She always did.

Betty smiled at her, though her eyes were still a bit hooked, and slid onto the second to last seat in the back row. Sam sat beside her, and Iris glanced around for another seat. People truly filled the room, and a blip of anxiety flowed through her when she realized this really was a fully-booked cruise. The room probably held fifty people—and the only seat which remained was up front, next to a man who was so wide he practically filled both seats.

Iris went that way, because the man at the front of the room was watching her, clearly waiting for her to sit before he began. She'd never been as grateful for her petite frame as she was when she slid in beside the tattooed military man.

His hair reminded her of dark roast coffee, and his tan skin testified that he spent plenty of time out in the Hawaiian sun. He flicked his black-as-coal eyes in her direction, and she tried a smile on her face.

Surprisingly, his lips twitched upward in return, and Iris focused on what the man up front was saying. "This is a great time for whale-watching," he said. "And there's a pod of humpbacks that have been seen every day for the past couple of weeks." He glanced around with a huge smile on his face. "We should see those later today. We'll dock tonight at Maui, but we won't be getting off. We leave port in the middle of the night to sail around the island to Lanai. We will disembark in Maui on the way back."

Blah blah blah. Iris had seen the map of the cruise. She knew where she was going and when the boat would stop and where she could get off. She relaxed now that she was here, the cares and worries of her landscaping business somewhere in her past.

"Our last stop is north of the Hawaiian Island chain, at a group of islands that are rumored to convert even the most unlucky in love."

Iris perked up then. This line of mystery islands intrigued her, and she couldn't wait until day nine, when they arrived there.

"Several people got marooned there in the seventies," the man continued. "And five couples ended up getting married by the pilot who happened to be a priest."

"That's so romantic," Iris sighed, wishing they could get off and explore the island.

The guy next to her that was practically sitting in her lap scoffed, and Iris's eyes flew to him. "You don't think it's romantic?" she whispered.

His dark eyes sparkled like dangerous stars. "No," he muttered. "It's not even true."

"How do you know?"

"I served in the military," he said needlessly, as if

his precise haircut, folded arms, and hint of his dog tag necklace didn't already tell her all of that.

The man up front went on to talk about things that were left behind when the couples got rescued, and how the islands were submerged in the fall and early winter when the rains came.

"So buddy up," he said. "You don't have to share rooms, but we want to make sure everyone has someone else on the cruise accountable for them."

Iris felt like she'd been transported back to fifth grade, when teams were being picked for kickball. Not particularly athletic, she never got chosen until the very end. Eden, her older sister, was the athletic one. The one teaching everyone about outdoor survival, the one who knew exactly how to hike, where to look for food, all of it.

She glanced around, noticing that people had already paired up around her.

Everyone but the tattooed meathead who didn't have a romantic bone in his body.

"I guess it's me and you," he said. He didn't look happy about the pairing at all.

"I guess," she said, still looking around. If Ivy were here, she'd know exactly how to charm this guy. But her twin had literally gotten all the flirting and talking genes, and Iris just stood there like she'd lost her ability to speak.

"Now that we're ready," the man said into the

microphone. "Check in with your buddy, and let's get on the ship."

It seemed like all forty-eight other people under the tent moved as a single unit, and Iris accepted the fact that she'd have to report to this Marine from time to time over the next fourteen days.

"I'm Iris McLaughlin," she said as they joined the line to check in and board.

"Justin Brunner," he said, and even his name sounded angry.

Iris sighed, trying to make it a quiet one. She didn't succeed as Justin looked at her with raised eyebrows. "You're not looking forward to the cruise?"

"No, I am." Betty and Sam had disappeared, and the vacation she'd been dreaming of vanished right before her eyes. "You?"

"No," he said. "This isn't really my scene."

"Why are you here then?" And alone too. Of course, she was alone as well. Sort of.

"Work," he said, stepping forward.

"Is that all I get? Work?" Iris wasn't sure where the sass had come from. He certainly wasn't the type of man to appreciate sarcasm, and the glare he gave her solidified that.

"I'm developing an app for this cruise line," he said coolly, handing the woman his ticket and adding, "Iris McLaughlin and I are partners."

"Welcome to Cruise Hawaii," the woman said with

the fakest smile on the planet. Justin smiled back, but it also radiated more of a chill than anything else.

Iris handed her ticket to the woman, got the same spiel, and headed for the boat, once again the last one to make it up the walkway to the ship.

Her nerves attacked, and her feet froze before she got on the ship. *Go on*, she told herself, especially when Justin turned back, an inquisitive look on his face.

The boat horn sounded, and she was going to get left behind if she didn't get on the vessel right now.

"Come on," Justin said, sudden compassion in his eyes. He reached for her, and she put her hand in his as a woman on the dock yelled at her to go.

Her skin tingled as Justin all but hauled her onto the boat, the gangplank got removed, and the boat pulled away from the dock. Her legs trembled, and she lurched, falling right into Justin, who certainly had the strength in his arms to catch her.

Oh, they're buddied up... Exciting! I can't wait to find out what happens next! **THE OVERBOARD MISTAKE is available now.**

The Perfect Storm (Book 1): A freak storm has her sliding down the mountain...right into the arms of her ex. As Eden and Holden spend time out in the wilds of Hawaii trying to survive, their old flame is rekindled. But with secrets and old feelings in the way, will Holden be able to take all the broken pieces of his life and put them back together in a way that makes sense? Or will he lose his heart and the reputation of his company because of a single landslide?

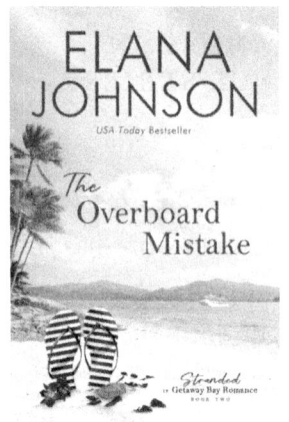

The Overboard Mistake (Book 2): Friends who ditch her. A pod of killer whales. A limping cruise ship. All reasons Iris finds herself stranded on an deserted island with the handsome Navy SEAL...

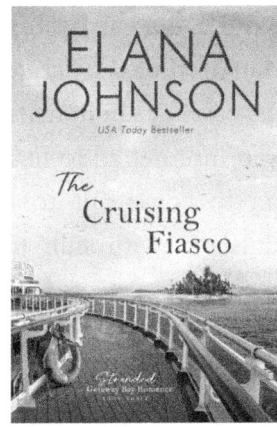

The Cruising Fiasco (Book 3): He can throw a precision pass, but he's dead in the water in matters of the heart...

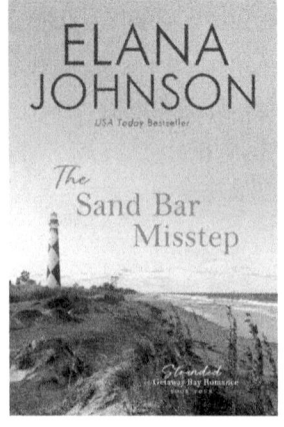

The Sand Bar Misstep (Book 4): Tired of the dating scene, a cowboy billionaire puts up an Internet ad to find a woman to come out to a deserted island with him to see if they can make a love connection...

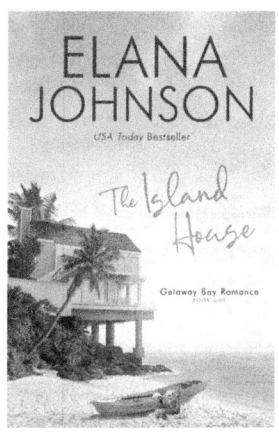

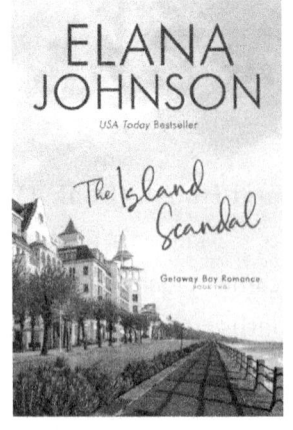

The Island Scandal (Book 2): Ashley Fox has known three things since age twelve: she was an excellent seam-stress, what her wedding would look like, and that she'd never leave the island of Getaway Bay. Now, at age 35, she's been right about two of them, at least.

Can Burke and Ash find a way to navigate a romance when they've only ever been friends?

The Island Hideaway (Book 3): She's 37, single (except for the cat), and a synchronized swimmer looking to make some extra cash. Pathetic, right? She thinks so, and she's going to spend this summer housesitting a cliff-side hideaway and coming up with a plan to turn her life around.

Can Noah and Zara fight their feelings for each other as easily as they trade jabs? Or will this summer shape up to be the one that provides the romance they've each always wanted?

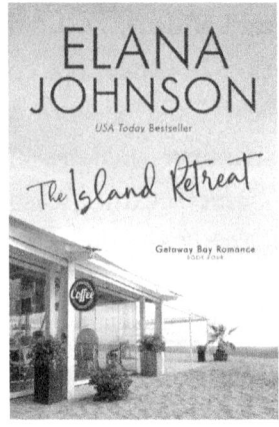

The Island Retreat (Book 4): Shannon's 35, divorced, and the highlight of her day is getting to the coffee shop before the morning rush. She tells herself that's fine, because she's got two cats and a past filled with emotional abuse. But she might be ready to heal so she can retreat into the arms of a man she's known for years...

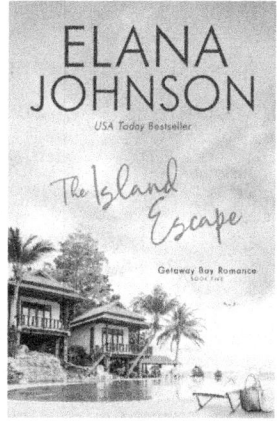

The Island Escape (Book 5): Riley Randall has spent eight years smiling at new brides, being excited for her friends as they find Mr. Right, and dating by a strict set of rules that she never breaks. But she might have to consider bending those rules ever so slightly if she wants an escape from the island...

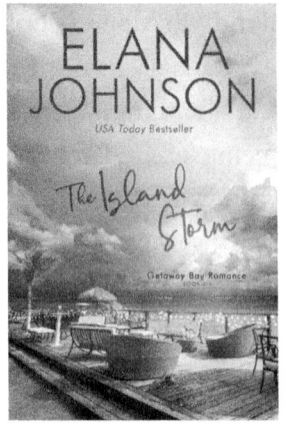

The Island Storm (Book 6): Lisa is 36, tired of the dating scene in Getaway Bay, and practically the only wedding planner at her company that hasn't found her own happy-ever-after. She's tried dating apps and blind dates...but could the company party put a man she's known for years into the spotlight?

The Island Wedding (Book 7): Deirdre is almost 40, estranged from her teenaged daughter, and determined not to feel sorry for herself. She does the best she can with the cards life has dealt her and she's dreaming of another island wedding...but it certainly can't happen with the widowed Chief of Police.

Getaway Bay (Book 2): Can Esther deal with dozens of business tasks, unhappy tourists, *and* the twists and turns in her new relationship?

Women's Beach Club (Book 3): With the help of her friends in the Beach Club, can Tawny solve the mystery, stay safe, and keep her man?

Straw and Diamonds (Book 4): Can Sasha maintain her sanity amidst their busy schedules, her issues with men like Jasper, and her desires to take her business to the next level?

The Billionaire Club (Book 5): Can Lexie keep her business affairs in the shadows while she brings her relationship out of them? Or will she have to confess everything to her new friends...and Jason?

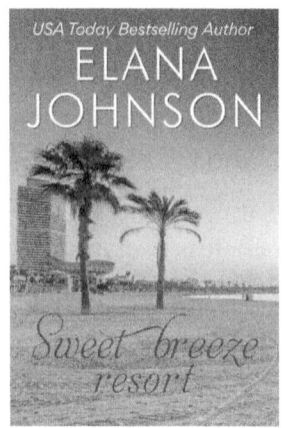

Sweet Breeze Resort (Book 6): Can Gina manage her business across the sea and finish the remodel at Sweet Breeze, all while developing a meaningful relationship with Owen and his sons?

Rainforest Retreat (Book 7): As their paths continue to cross and Lawrence and Maizee spend more and more time together, will he find in her a retreat from all the family pressure? Can Maizee manage her relationship with her boss, or will she once again put her heart—and her job—on the line?

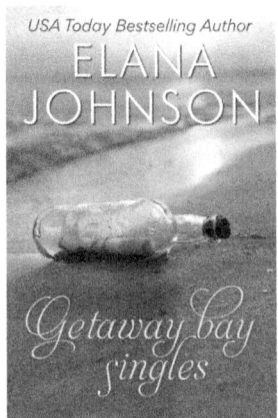

Getaway Bay Singles (Book 8): Can Katie bring him into her life, her daughter's life, and manage her business while he manages the app? Or will everything fall apart for a second time?

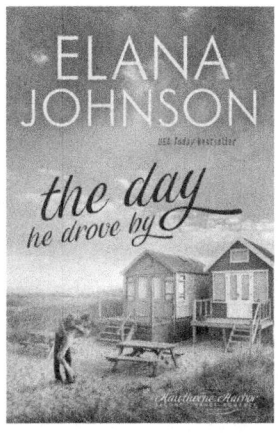

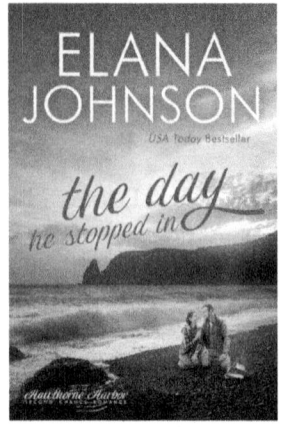

The Day He Stopped In (Hawthorne Harbor Second Chance Romance, Book 2): Janey Germaine is tired of entertaining tourists in Olympic National Park all day and trying to keep her twelve-year-old son occupied at night. When longtime friend and the Chief of Police, Adam Herrin, offers to take the boy on a ride-along one fall evening, Janey starts to see him in a different light. Do they have the courage to take their relationship out of the friend zone?

The Day He Said Hello (Hawthorne Harbor Second Chance Romance, Book 3): Bennett Patterson is content with his boring firefighting job and his big great dane...until he comes face-toface with his high school girlfriend, Jennie Zimmerman, who swore she'd never return to Hawthorne Harbor. Can they rekindle their old flame? Or will their opposite personalities keep them apart?

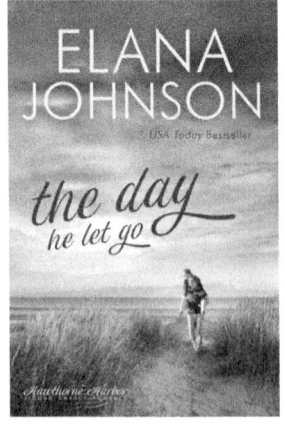

The Day He Let Go (Hawthorne Harbor Second Chance Romance, Book 4): Trent Baker is ready for another relationship, and he's hopeful he can find someone who wants him and to be a mother to his son. Lauren Michaels runs her own general contract company, and she's never thought she has a maternal bone in her body. But when she gets a second chance with the handsome K9 cop who blew her off when she first came to town, she can't say no... Can Trent and Lauren make their differences into strengths and build a family?

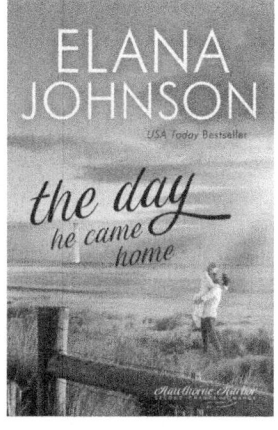

The Day He Came Home (Hawthorne Harbor Second Chance Romance, Book 5): A wounded Marine returns to Hawthorne Harbor years after the woman he was married to for exactly one week before she got an annulment...and then a baby nine months later. Can Hunter and Alice make a family out of past heartache?

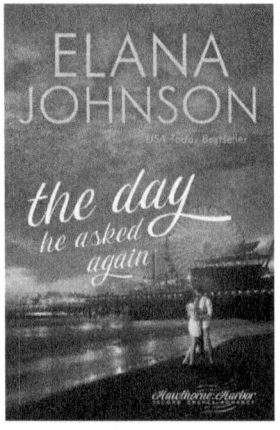

The Day He Asked Again (Hawthorne Harbor Second Chance Romance, Book 6): A Coast Guard captain would rather spend his time on the sea...unless he's with the woman he's been crushing on for months. Can Brooklynn and Dave make their second chance stick?

ABOUT ELANA

Elana Johnson is the USA Today bestselling author of dozens of clean and wholesome contemporary romance novels. She lives in Utah, where she mothers two fur babies, works full-time with her husband, and eats a lot of veggies while writing. Find her on her website at elanajohnson.com.

Printed in Great Britain
by Amazon

23351654R00106